Finding the Best Life

Print ISBN: 9798985850574

Ebook ISBN: 9798985850567

Cover by GetCovers

Trigger warnings:

This book contains content that some readers may find offensive and/or triggering. Included in this are:

Religious Trauma

Suicidal ideologies and suicide

Frequent use of adult language

Frequent sexually explicit scenes

Rape

For every person that has found their
way free from a high control group, and
for all those still trying.

Author's Note

I was born and raised in the Jehovah's Witness cult. In this story I have tried to remain true to the teachings and beliefs as they were when I was a member. I have been free for well over a decade, and in that time some of their teachings have changed.

Most recently they have begun allowing the men to wear beards, the women to wear pants, and their members to clink glasses and say 'cheers'.

Some things, however, remain the same:

They are a patriarchal, high control group. Women, while allowed to have a small role, are not allowed to be leaders in the congregation.

They still hold to their shunning policy, which they call 'Disfellowshipping'. I was disfellowshipped in 2008. As a disfellowshipped individual, every member of the Jehovah's Witness organization is required to shun me, including family and lifelong friends. If they do not, then they too could find themselves shunned.

And while they now allow members to take certain parts of blood, blood transfusions are still against their beliefs and will result in the person who accepts one being shunned.

Since walking away from the cult, I have lived a much happier and more fulfilling life than I could have ever imagined while in. In 2021 I published my first book, 'The Brotherhood of Time: Dawn', a Young Adult time travel adventure that contains an LGBTQIA+ storyline that I would have never been allowed to write as a member of the cult.

For as long as I can remember, the written word has been an escape for me, whether it was reading the works of others, or writing my own stories. When I was younger, it was my escape from an abusive home. I now enjoy sharing my stories with the world.

While the teachings and beliefs in this story are intended to be an accurate representation of the Jehovah's Witnesses teachings, the story itself, and the characters within, are my own creation and do not represent any actual persons, living or dead.

It is my hope that you will enjoy Emily's journey as she finds her way free of the cult. None of us have perfect lives, and her character is no different. However, on her journey she will begin learn who her authentic self is and take steps toward finding *her* best life.

1

I'll never forget the first time that I saw him. It was nearing the end of our lunch break on the second day of the 'Give God Glory' District Convention of Jehovah's Witnesses, July 12, 2003 in Cleveland, Ohio.

It was always exciting going to the convention, and since I was nineteen and still not dating anyone, I also had the added excitement of looking for a good christian Brother to date.

"Who is that talking to Miguel," I asked as I linked my arm into Rebecca's.

Rebecca, two years older than me, rolled her eyes. "That's Antony. He's from Sandusky, I think. Miguel likes him, but I think he's kind of a jerk. He is also," she said, stopping and looking at me, "twenty-six. A bit old for you."

I looked at her and smiled playfully. "I was just wondering; I've never seen him before."

She didn't look convinced. As we approached, her brother Miguel saw us and smiled.

"Sis! Emily," he said, waving at us.

I quickly gave Miguel a hug. I was 5' 8" and wearing short heels, but I still had to stretch to reach him. Miguel stood 6'5" and was in fantastic shape. You wouldn't know it, but under that baggy suit was a very chiseled body.

Ever since I had discovered that boys were actually, in fact, not 'icky', I had had a crush on him. He was Rebecca's older brother, twenty-three, and he had always looked at me like his little sister.

I breathed him in as I made sure not to let the hug linger too long. He smelled like Curve cologne and whatever body wash he had used that morning.

I stepped back and smiled at him, trying to make sure I didn't get lost in his perfect hazel eyes. Easily the most eligible Brother in our area: tall, perfect olive complexion, his hair just long enough to not be considered 'rebellious' and a smile to die for. How he was still single I couldn't understand.

"Em, this is my friend, Antony," he said gesturing to the man I had noticed earlier. "Antony, this is Becca's best friend Emily. She's like a second sister."

His words broke my heart a little, but I was used to it. I had learned a long time ago to hide my feelings around him.

"A pleasure to meet you," I said, shaking Antony's hand with a smile.

Antony was a bit on the nerdy side, but the cool nerdy. He wore large rimmed glasses, and while not as tall as Miguel, he had to be at least six foot tall. His curly brown hair hung perfectly around his face. His chin sported just a little bit of stubble, as if he hadn't shaved this morning.

"The pleasure is all mine."

His smooth, deep voice pulled me in. While he wasn't unattractive, he certainly wasn't the most handsome Brother I had ever seen.

But that voice. My hormones decided that that voice was going to send a flutter to my heart and further south, and I stood a little straighter.

"Nice to see you again, Rebecca," he said, shaking my friends' hand.

"You too, Antony. We really should be getting back to our seats though. Maybe we'll be able to catch up after the program," she said, not bothering to wait for an answer as she once again linked our arms and practically dragged me away.

"Or you guys could come sit with us for the afternoon program," Antony suggested.

"Maybe," she said without looking back.

"You really don't like him," I giggled.

"He's stuck up. And besides, we don't need him getting any ideas about either of us."

I was born and raised as one of Jehovah's Witnesses. When I was twelve, I made the decision to get baptized and officially become a member. By fourteen I had decided to make the door-to-door ministry my focus, and had signed up to become a pioneer, devoting ninety hours a month in the door-to-door ministry.

Rebecca and her family had started attending our Kingdom Hall right after I was baptized. Her dad was an elder, and her mom a pioneer.

But she was known to be a little bit worldly, people around our congregation gossiping that her dad shouldn't be allowed to be an elder because of the way she behaved.

Nothing crazy of course, but even though she was only fourteen at the time, she was known to be a flirt. Always trying to hang around with the older boys in the congregation, she had developed a reputation.

Miguel had moved out of the family home right before they came to our congregation, but they were close, especially after her dad died, and he was always around.

"I don't know, with that voice, I have a couple of ideas of my own," I giggled again as I trailed off before finishing the sentence.

As I had gotten older, even though I knew it was wrong, I had discovered masturbation. My parents had never had 'the talk' with me, and with Rebecca being a little older than me, she was the one that I had went to as I started to get curious. She helped me to figure out what exactly I liked.

Rebecca just shook her head. When we got back to our section Rebecca asked her mom if we could sit with Miguel. It was normal for us to try to sit with other families, breaking the monotony of it all was one of the best parts of the convention.

"Oh hunny," her mom said, glancing at her watch, "there's only fifteen minutes before the music starts.

Are you going to be able to be in your seats by then?"

"Of course, mom, this place isn't that big."

She was right. The Cleveland State University Convocation Center wasn't tiny, but there were only two levels and today's attendance was just over 7,000 people.

"Emily," her mom said, turning to me. "You don't think your parent's would care, do you?"

My parents hadn't been able to make the convention this year. Mom was getting sicker, and Dad was trying his best to take care of her. Rebecca's mom had volunteered to take me and record the program for them.

I shook my head. "No, I'm sure they wouldn't."

"Okay, go on then, get to your seat's quick," she said with a shooing motion.

Without another word, we scooped up our books, and I grabbed the blanket that I had brought because I was always cold in the arena.

We made our way to the section that Miguel was sitting in, but we didn't see him anywhere. Before I could say anything, Antony waved at us.

"Oh, there's Antony," I said as I climbed the stairs to where he was.

"You guys come to sit with us," he asked with a smile, his voice again warming me.

Rebecca gave him a look. "No, we came to sit with my brother, but since you're with him I guess we'll have to deal with you too."

Just then, Miguel turned the corner and started up the stairs, smiling wide when he saw us.

"Hey! You with us for the afternoon?"

I smiled back at him. Even though I was pretty sure he was asking his sister, I answered.

"Yeah, I'm hoping it's warmer over here. I was freezing all morning," I said as I held up my blanket.

"Well, you can sit next to me," Antony said quickly.

I smiled and tried to keep eye contact with him, but I looked away before I blushed.

"Yeah, better her than me," Rebecca mumbled.

A Brother walked onto the stage in the middle of the arena and announced that the program would start soon. A few minutes later, he asked everyone who was able to stand and sing the opening song for the afternoon.

I wasn't prepared for how well Antony could sing. That deep, silky voice made me shiver, and my thoughts were anything but clean as the song ended.

I said a quick prayer, and sat down. I was at a spiritual banquet, and I needed to focus on the program and not the man sitting next to me.

"You want your blanket," he whispered. "You looked cold during the song, I noticed you shivered."

My blanket and extra books had been set in a seat on the other side of him, so I nodded and he handed it to me, his rough hand brushing mine.

I managed to ignore the thoughts that had been trying to get in since I met Antony. The next two speakers had my full attention. Until I felt him nudge my arm.

"Hey, can I share a little of the blanket with you?"

I nodded and tried to whisper "yes" but I'm not entirely sure it was audible.

He smiled as he took the edge of the blanket and pulled some of it over himself. A few moments later, our shoulders were touching, and I could have sworn I felt his hand brush my thigh for just a split second.

2

Antony leaned into me. I felt his hand clearly on my thigh now, rubbing and slowly moving up. I was trying to focus on the speaker, trying to remind myself that I was at the convention and that this wasn't appropriate.

I knew that I should stop him, at the very least excuse myself and walk away. But the flutter in my underwear was hard to ignore as his hand slid further up.

I looked over, trying to be nonchalant, and his face betrayed none of what his hand was doing. He looked as though he was intently focused on the speaker.

I tried to be the same, but I was sure I wasn't as convincing. His hand made its way up to my hip and slid inward, only the thin cotton of my dress and underwear separating his fingers from my lips. He rubbed, the feeling of his hand causing me to catch my breath suddenly. I coughed, trying to hide my small gasp.

Antony smiled and slipped out of the blanket. I wrapped the blanket tighter around myself and focused on the stage, trying not to watch as he left his bible and notebook on the chair when he walked away.

Viking Lodge, 1:15 was written on the top page of his notebook. The Viking Lodge was a private meeting area where the Brothers met at certain times during the program to discuss behind the scenes tasks. I knew that he was working in the parking department with Miguel for the convention.

Was this the time he had to be at one of the meetings, or was it instructions for me? I glanced at my watch. 1:15 was only ten minutes from now. I sat there for another five of those minutes paying no attention to what the speaker was saying, my mind racing with ideas of what might happen if I met him.

I finally stood, grabbed my clutch, and left the auditorium. I slipped into the restroom and checked my hair and put on a little lip gloss. I wasn't allowed to wear makeup, but I got away with lip gloss because it was also a moisturizer. I quickly made my way to the service elevator that the Brothers all took to get to the Viking Lodge.

"Sister Marquette," the older Brother at the elevator greeted me as I walked up. He was from a neighboring congregation, but I couldn't remember his name just now.

"How is your mom," he asked, standing as I approached.

"She's holding on."

He smiled that smile that people had started giving me ever since my mom's illness became known. "I'll keep her in my prayers," he said.

"Thank you."

I didn't ask him why, since everyone's prayers were doing nothing to help her health. It was just what you say to people when they are going through a hard time, as if your prayers can do anything to actually help.

"Is it time for the pioneer meeting already," he asked, pulling out an old pocket watch from his suit.

"No, I offered to help get the room set up."

"Of course," he smiled as he eyed me. "You're a good young Sister. You'll make some Brother an excellent christian wife one day."

I just smiled as he lifted the door to the elevator. Why did it feel like the old men in the congregation were always being just a bit creepy?

He got in with me and closed the door, hitting the button.

"Make sure you tell your parents I said hello," he said as the elevator stopped and he opened the door.

"I will, thank you."

I stepped off and he closed the door. Hearing the whirring of the elevator going back down, I looked around but saw no one.

Maybe I was wrong about what the note had said. I walked around the room, my mind imagining all of the things I had hoped might happen when I got here. I was just about to call the elevator back when a hand spun me around.

"I hoped you would read my note," Antony said, as he wrapped an arm around my waist and pulled me to him.

"I…yes, well…what are you doing?"

He brought his lips to my ear, his warm breath tickling my neck. "What do you want me to do?"

I thought his voice was irresistible before. But in a whisper, this close to me? I tipped my head to the side, opening my neck.

"I want you to kiss me," I whispered back, dropping my clutch to the ground.

His lips on my neck sent a lightning bolt of pleasure to my core, and a moan escaped me.

He must have sensed my concern at the sudden sound. "The room is basically soundproof, and no one should be here for at least a half hour."

I twined my fingers in his curls. "What if someone comes up?"

His lips worked their way to my collar bone. "Then we will hear the elevator," he said in between kisses.

I pulled him back and brought his lips to mine. I kissed him slowly at first, but when his lips parted my tongue probed his eagerly.

Picking me up easily, he set me down on one of the desks in the room. I spread my legs and pulled him close, our lips never parting.

I could feel his bulge pressing against my dress. How many times had I touched myself, dreaming of a moment like this with a man? I always got lost in how it would feel and what I would do. But now, there was no more thinking.

There was only raw desire putting my body on autopilot.

I reached down and gripped him through his suit pants. God, it felt so thick. He moaned and kissed between my breasts.

Using one hand, I slipped my top and bra strap from my shoulder, and he quickly had my nipple in his mouth. He teased and sucked on it while I began grinding my hips against his.

Gently he pulled on my skin with his teeth and I let out a loud moan. He began working his hands down my body, until he slid them up my skirt.

Higher, and higher they went, slowly running across my smooth thighs. His hands felt so good that I nearly begged him to go faster.

He pulled his face back and looked at me just as his fingertips reached the edges of my thong.

"Do you want me to stop," he asked, his voice husky and hungry.

I spread my legs wider and pulled him back to me, kissing him with all the passion I had. I had only kissed a few other boys, and I wasn't sure that I really was any good, but the lust in his eyes told me I was doing something right.

I gasped as his fingers moved the thin cotton of my underwear to the side and he began massaging my wet slit, his finger tracing my clit before slipping inside of me

"Fuck, you're so wet," he said. The curse so at odds with anything I expected to hear this weekend, and I almost felt bad about what we were doing and where we were doing it. Almost.

"And you're so fucking hard," I answered back as I grabbed his cock through his pants.

He slipped another finger inside of me. "I want to feel your hand on me," he said as he slowly slid his fingers in and out of me.

I fumbled for his belt and zipper, and when I finally had him in my hand I was ready to let him have every part of me.

I was a virgin, but I had used my toy so many times that I needed to feel a real man inside of me.

He pulled his fingers slowly from me and brought them to his lips. Looking me in the eyes, he licked my taste off of them.

Without a word he slipped my thong off and pushed my knees wide apart, kissing the inside of my thigh, slowly moving his tongue up higher and higher.

Just as his tongue touched my clit, the elevator began moving.

3

As soon as we heard the sound of the elevator, we sprang into action. Antony jumped back and quickly redressed himself.

I followed suit, pulling my bra and top back into place. I picked up my purse and grabbed an empty chair, moving it aimlessly, hoping that it would look like I was busy.

Seconds before the door opened, my heart stopped. Antony was near where he had set me on the desk.

"My thong," I hissed and pointed at my underwear laying a few feet from him. He smoothly picked them up and put them in his jacket.

"Brother Householder," a surprised voice came when the door finally opened.

"Brother Jackson," Antony said quickly. "We were just setting up for the pioneer meeting."

I almost laughed. His last name was 'Householder'? The irony.

"Hi, I'm Emily," I smiled at the man who had just entered, shaking his hand.

"Marcus," he answered with a smile. "Your parents are John and Tammy, right?"

I know that I reddened when I realized that he knew my family. At least of them.

Really my mother's name was 'Tam Myung-Hee' before she married my father, and since it was easier in America she just went by Tammy.

"Yes, that's them. Have we met?"

"No, no," the older man said. "I used to be friends with your father ages ago, but I haven't seen them in years. My wife and I have been keeping your mother in our prayers though. She has been an excellent example in the congregation for a long time."

I mumbled a simple 'thank you' and excused myself. I couldn't handle hearing any more about how great my mom was.

I was aware of how amazing she is, and it's not fair that at only forty-two years old she's fighting for her life.

Prayers were doing nothing to make her better, and the next person that talked about her like she was already gone might make me say something I shouldn't.

As I rode the elevator back down, tears bit at the corners of my eyes. It was hard being the dutiful little Jehovah's Witness girl. I was expected to just have faith, listen to the elders, and keep following their rules.

It was getting more and more difficult to do that. Watching my mother weaken and wither before my eyes, while the Brothers and Sisters at the Kingdom Hall offered their empty sympathies was doing nothing to help me have faith.

Why would Jehovah let my mother, 'an excellent example in the congregation', get sick and die slowly in front of my eyes?

I stepped outside and took a deep breath of fresh air. Or, at least as fresh as it could be in downtown Cleveland. I felt my phone vibrate, and I pulled it from my clutch.

Beccs: Where r u

Shit.

Me: Stepped out for some air. I was cold and losing focus. Be back soon.

I knew if I sat back down under the blanket with Antony I would not behave myself.

Unknown number: Hey, r u coming back soon? Ive got something you might want to put back on…

A thrill ran down my spine. My thong. Oh. My. God. He has my fucking thong.

Beccs: Gave Antony ur # cuz he was worried ur not back yet

Beccs: Didn't think you'd mind ;)

Antony: I can bring them to you somewhere if you want.

Fuck. Fuck, fuck, fuck. Okay I can do this. It was a mistake, I'll pray about it later.

What is he thinking, that he's going to give them to me in the middle of the arena?

Me to Beccs: k

Me to Antony: Where could you possibly give them to me in there?

The idea of him walking around with my thong in his pocket sent a thrill through me. What the hell was I doing? I'm not this easy.

I've been the perfect little Witness my whole life, this can't be happening. But, goddamn did I want him between my legs again.

Antony: Who said anything about in here? Meet me at the garage you and Rebecca parked in.

Bad idea, Emily. Bad idea. But so good too.

Me: Be there in ten.

I would just get my underwear back and walk back to the convention. Maybe Jehovah would forgive me if I pay close attention.

Antony: ;) see u there.

Antony: Level 3

I walked quickly to the garage. I tried so hard to focus on praying for forgiveness for what we did, but I couldn't stop thinking about the details.

I replayed the feeling of his lips on my neck, our tongues exploring each other's mouth; his tongue on my clit for just the briefest moment before we were interrupted.

By the time I got to the third floor of the garage, I was wet and wishing that I could feel Antony's skin on mine again.

4

I exited the stairwell and stepped into the parking garage. It was hot and stuffy, and I looked around hoping that Antony would be there soon.

"Looking for these?"

I paused for just a second at the sound of that perfect voice, then turned to see Antony holding my underwear just inside the stairwell.

"Jesus, give those here before someone sees," I said as I practically ran to grab them.

Before I could get the tiny bit of black lace that he held, he pulled them up and put them to his nose, breathing my scent deeply.

"I want to taste you again."

I should have been mortified. That action should have been one that was embarrassing to me. I should have turned red and run, never talking to him again. I didn't.

"Why smell that, when you can put your face between my legs again?"

I surprised myself with my own lack of inhibition, but we'd already started something. I could pray for forgiveness when we finished what we started.

"Where," he asked, his succulent voice husky with need.

I didn't have the keys to Rebecca's car, and it was barely big enough to sit in comfortably anyway. Shit. I shrugged.

"I don't know."

He smiled. "Well, I was thinking on the way over here that my Hummer isn't far. And I booked a room for the weekend. So, depending on how long you think we can be away…" his voice trailed off.

Both ideas thrilled me, but I knew that we had limited time. I snatched my thong away from him and pulled it on, savoring as his eyes followed to see my wetness before I covered it.

"Car. Then you can take these back off."

A thrill ran through me. What was I doing? This was crazy. I could say we made a mistake in the Viking Lodge, but this? This wasn't a mistake. This was me giving in to what I wanted, even though I knew I shouldn't. And it thrilled me.

He took off up the stairs. I struggled to keep up in my heels, so I pulled them off and chased him. He stopped at the fifth floor and looked at me.

As soon as I had caught up to him he grabbed me and kissed me. Hungry, lustful, needy, urgent, his tongue probed mine. I bit his lip as he ran his hand under my top and teased my nipple through my thin bra. I pushed him back.

"Where is your truck?"

He smiled and pulled a remote from his pocket, giving me a perfect view of the bulge I had created in his pants. I heard a 'chirp chirp', and I ran to the sound. I giggled as he scooped me up from behind and ran with me in his arms.

He set me down facing the door of his Hummer. As he kissed my neck, his hand ran up my skirt, stopping as he reached my ass. His finger slid my thong to the side and slipped inside of me.

"You're so fucking wet. God you are perfect."

I pushed my ass back towards him and he rubbed his thumb on my forbidden hole. Fuck, I'd tried using toys on that myself, but I never liked the way it felt. But now, with his thumb doing the work…I let out a moan and he spun me around.

Reaching back I pulled the door handle, and in an instant he had me on the back seat and the door closed. The dark tint might hide what we were doing, but if anyone walked by the rocking of the truck would surely give it away.

He kissed me deeply as he spread my legs apart, his rough hands giving me a thrill on my thighs. He backed up and looked me in the eyes as he lowered his mouth to my wet underwear. He kissed me through the thin cotton and I arched my back.

"Stop teasing."

That was all the encouragement that he needed. He slid the fabric to the side and slipped his middle finger into me as far as it would go.I moaned as he slowly worked the finger in and out, his tongue matching the rhythm on my clit.

Fuck, how many times had I dreamed about something like this as I touched myself? And here it was happening. A man I just met, at a place where I was supposed to be learning about God. The absolute dirtiness of it had my body trembling. I could feel myself getting close.

"Yes, yes, don't stop," I begged as I held his head against me.

He moved faster, his tongue lashing my clit, and he added a second finger. The feeling of his fingers stretching me as his tongue soaked me in drove me over the edge. I undulated in rhythm with his fingers until I went rigid, back arched, a moan loud and free coming out of my lips as he made my other lips quiver.

He pulled his face back and smiled at me, slowly removing his fingers. I wanted more so badly.

"You taste amazing," he said.

I was too surprised to stop him as he came up and kissed me. I had tasted my fingers before and never really liked it. But again, on his lips, with him, I loved the way I tasted.

I pushed him back and sat him down. He smiled as I fumbled with his zipper and belt.

"You want some help," he asked with a smirk.

But it was too late, and before he could say anything else, I had my lips around his rock-hard cock. The moan that came from him was like fuel to my fire. I slowly worked my mouth up and down his shaft, going a little bit deeper each time.

It had been years since the one time I had done this, and I never thought I would again after the guilt I had felt. But fuck the guilt, I needed to feel him in my mouth, to taste him.

He was so thick, and my mouth stretched as I took him in. Soon, my throat stretched to let his full length invade it.

Faster and faster I took him, stopping at the head before sliding it back into my throat.

"Oh fuck, I'm going to come," that deep voice practically yelled out.

I didn't stop. I took every inch of him as I felt him start to quiver. I gently squeezed his balls and he exploded. I swallowed every drop as I slowed my pace, still sucking him until he told me to stop.

"It's too sensitive."

The truck was hot, it smelled like sex, and I couldn't think straight. My head was spinning as I climbed on top of him, straddling him.

"I don't have a condom," he said hesitantly.

I knew he had just come, I knew I should not be that close to him even with my birth control, but my wetness needed to feel him. I slid my lips up and down his shaft.

"Tell me to stop," I said, looking him in the eye as I moved my hips.

He shook his head.

"What do you want," I asked, wanting, needing to hear his perfect voice say it.

"To be inside of you."

I stopped sliding on him and grabbed his cock. Still so hard. I held it as I sat myself down on it, feeling the tip spread my lips apart.

5

I slowly slid down his shaft, holding his face in my hands and looking him in the eyes as I felt all of him touch places no one ever had. When I reached the bottom, I leaned in and kissed him.

"Tell me to stop," I said again, as I started to rise.

When only his head was left inside of me, he grabbed my hips and thrust his full length back into me.

"No, don't stop."

The feeling of him suddenly in me again sent a fresh lightning bolt of pleasure through me and I shuddered. I leaned back against the front seat and ground my hips back and forth against him, feeling him stretch me in ways my toys never had.

The look in his eyes was nothing short of carnal. "Do you like the way my pussy feels wrapped around your cock," I asked, surprising myself again.

Who was I right now? I didn't know, but I knew I felt more free than I ever had.

"Fuck it's so tight. You're going to make me come again if you don't slow down."

I did slow down, pulling my top off and releasing my bra. His eyes drank me in greedily. His look made me wild. I was no longer in control, my body was making its own decisions.

I buried his cock inside of me and leaned forward, taking his face in my hands and kissing him. I could still taste myself on his lips and it drove me crazy.

"I want to feel you come," I said, grinding my hips against him without pulling up.

I thought he was going to push me off for a second, but the look in his eyes told me he wanted this as bad as I did. I rocked back and forth on him, faster and faster.

"Fuck," he said, tipping his head back.

I grabbed his head. "No, look at me when you cum."

He obeyed, and as his cock started to twitch I took his hands and put them on my bare breasts. He squeezed and massaged my nipples as he moaned.

"Oh fuck," he yelled out, and I felt the heat of him deep inside of me.

But I didn't get up. I was too close to my own release, and a moment later I pulled his mouth to my nipple and dug my nails into the back of his neck soaking his back seat as I came.

A few minutes later, we were dressed and walking back to the convention. Antony grabbed my hand and laced his fingers with mine. A fresh rush of blood ran through me at his skin on mine again.

"Do you want to get dinner with Miguel and I after the program," he asked without looking at me.

The thought sounded great; I loved the idea of more time with him.

"I would love to, but I have to go home with his mom and Becca."

He sighed and squeezed my hand. "Sit with us again tomorrow? Maybe we can plan dinner with Miguel and Becca for tomorrow evening."

I just smiled. "Maybe."

When we got back in view of the Convocation Center, I realized that someone might see me holding his hand and I slipped out of it quickly.

He smiled and tried to play it off, but I could hear the hurt in his voice.

"Embarrassed by me?"

"No, I just…we…someone," I struggled to form my thoughts into a sentence. "I just met you, and I don't want to deal with people gossiping because they saw us holding hands. But if we find a way to see more of each other…"

He smiled, and leaned in towards my ear. "I've seen all of you, but I'd love to see you again," he said in that husky, hungry voice.

I could feel myself flush with heat, and it took everything in me to not grab his hand and go back to his truck.

Becca: Where r u its been almost an hour

Becca's text pulled me out of my thoughts. God, had it been that long?

"Boyfriend," Antony asked playfully.

I wasn't feeling playful as a pit developed in my stomach at the thought of being found out.

"Becca," I said flatly. "She's wondering where I am."

Me: Outside. Don't feel good, be in soon.

"I'll go to the other entrance, so we don't walk back in together," he said, seeming to catch on to my concern.

I looked at him and couldn't help but smile. Holy shit, was I falling in love already?

"Okay, I'll see you in there."

I watched as he walked around the corner of the Convocation Center and out of sight. I sat down on one of the benches and felt the reminder of what we did still dripping out of me.

A moment of…regret? Guilt? Shame? I didn't know, but it started to hit just as I heard my name.

"Emily, there you are," Rebecca said, coming down towards me.

"Hey," I smiled weakly.

"Hey, you look a bit flushed. Are you okay?"

I shrugged. "I don't know. I wasn't feeling great, so I wanted to get some fresh air but I'm not sure I feel any better now."

She came and sat beside me, rubbing my back. When her hand passed over my bra strap I was reminded of how I had just had it off not ten minutes ago, Antony's face buried in my chest. Another wave of…whatever it was I was feeling struck.

"You don't look good. Come on, let's get you back inside. Maybe the air conditioning will help," she said standing and holding out her hand to help me up.

I took her hand and stood, linking arms and walking back in with her.

"What did I miss," I asked as we walked to the entrance.

She shrugged. "Not much, but I was only half paying attention because I was worried about you. There was a good talk on relying on Jehovah to help us through difficult times though. I thought it kind of applied to everything going on with your mom."

Oh god, my mom. She would be so disappointed in me. I'd been such a good daughter for so long. She didn't know how hard all of this was on me, watching her get sick, praying and praying but her not getting any better.

"Yeah," was all I could think to say.

The rest of the afternoon dragged on. We were on the last part of the program and Antony still hadn't returned to our seats. I kept replaying the day with him in my mind. A mixture of excitement, heat, and shame made my stomach churn.

What we did was so wrong. Right? It felt so good. Hell, it helped me think of something other than my problems for a while and that had to be a good thing, right?

After the final song and prayer of the day, I turned to Miguel.

"What happened to your friend," I asked him, trying to be casual.

"Antony? He had assignments this afternoon. I think he was on parking duty."

I was both relieved and disappointed that I wouldn't see him again today.

Rebecca looked at her phone.

"That's mom," she said to her brother. "She is going to stay and help clean, but I told her that Em isn't feeling good. Do you mind taking us home?"

Miguel looked conflicted. "I was supposed to help with trash cleanup and then go out to eat with Antony, but I'm sure I can let Brother Jones know I have a family issue and need to go. Antony will understand."

I smiled at him. "Thank you."

He pulled out his phone and began tapping out a text to, I assumed, Brother Jones.

"Okay," he said. "Done. Let's get our stuff and I'll get you home."

6

The ride home was quiet. I used the fact that I was 'sick' to my advantage, not talking to Rebecca and Miguel as he drove us down the interstate. That is until Miguel made me the center of the conversation.

"Hey, Emily," he said in his serious tone. "I noticed you seemed to like Antony, and he's my friend and everything, but like, he's probably not the best person for you to be hanging around with."

The nausea that I was already fighting bubbled up in my throat.

"I barely talked to him," I said, trying to be dismissive and hoping that would end it.

Rebecca chimed in. "Yeah, but you sure were cozied up to him under the blanket. And I saw how you looked at him earlier."

"Sorry I was being nice and sharing my blanket. He said he was cold, next time I'll tell him no," I snapped, a bit shorter than I meant to be. "And you're the one that gave him my number."

"You gave him her number," Miguel asked side eyeing his sister.

"Yeah, well she thought he was cute, and she could use a little bit of distraction right now."

"Hi, it's me, Emily, sitting right here while you discuss me like I've done something terrible," I said annoyed.

"No one is saying you did anything wrong," Miguel said, with another glance over at Rebecca. "He just has a bit of a…reputation. I know you didn't think anything of it, but he may have thought you were interested in him or something. I'm just saying, be careful around him."

"Reputation?"

Miguel sighed. "Look, he's my friend, and he's never been disfellowshipped. But he has been publicly reproved a few times. Everyone could guess why, he always seems to have a new young girl that he spends time with. And they don't always have a chaperone around. I'm just saying, I don't want people to talk about you."

Great. So, I had just given myself up like it was nothing to a guy who had a reputation for sleeping around. I guess my sin wasn't bad enough, it had to have no meaning either.

"Pull over," I said suddenly.

Miguel looked at me in the mirror. "What, now? We're on the highway."

"Pull over unless you want puke all over your car," I gritted out through my teeth.

He obliged, throwing on the hazards, and slowing quickly to the side of the road. I bolted out as soon as the car stopped and threw up my lunch in the grass on the side of the road.

Rebecca was next to me in an instant, holding my hair back. "Crap Em, are you okay? Maybe you should stay home tomorrow."

I coughed and spit. I just nodded. I didn't want to see Antony again, and this was the perfect excuse to stay away.

Except I did want to see him again, to feel his lips on mine, his fingers roaming my body before they...fuck these feelings were terrible. What had I gotten myself into?

Thankfully, they left me alone for the rest of the drive. I closed my eyes and tried to relax, but I just kept seeing Antony. Seeing the look in his eyes when he had seen me naked, that gaze that followed along as I had put my thong back on. His perfect voice when I asked what he wanted, and he had said 'to be inside of you'.

The heat of the memory was quickly tamped out by what Miguel had said. How many other girls had he said that to? How many other Sisters had thought that they were irresistible to him, just for him to take what he wanted and move on to the next?

No, if I never saw him again that would be perfect. I would pray and beg Jehovah to forgive me. I would tell the Elders in the congregation…no, no I wouldn't. That would devastate my parents and they had enough to deal with right now.

No, it was just one mistake. Jehovah would forgive me as long as I prayed and meant it. I would focus on his preaching work and pour myself into his service. He would forgive me.

I must have managed to doze off for at least a few minutes, because I woke up to Rebecca calling my name.

"Em. Em. Emily, we're here."

I opened my eyes and gave her a weak smile. "Sorry. Thank you for the ride home."

I got out of the car and Rebecca stepped out with me. She walked me silently up to the door. I unlocked it and hugged her, thanking her again.

"You're welcome. I'll let my mom know you probably won't be coming with us tomorrow. Just text me if you feel better and we can pick you up."

I stepped inside and closed the door. Dad was sitting in his chair, reading The Watchtower.

"Hey, Miguel called and said you weren't feeling well."

Of course he had. "I'm not. I got sick during the second half. How's mom?"

Dad's eyes darkened a little. "She had a rough day. She's sleeping now. We'll see what the Doctor say's on Monday."

I just nodded. "I'm going to lay down. I love you dad."

My father stood from his chair and walked towards the kitchen. "Do you want me to warm you up some dinner? It won't take but a minute."

There was no way that I could stomach food, just the thought made me nauseous again. "No thanks. I just want to rest."

I walked upstairs to my room and closed the door. After setting my bag down, I went into my bathroom and started to change. I felt unclean as I took off my clothes, my underwear with a stain where myself and Antony had dried.

I stepped into the shower and cried as the hot water washed away the remnants of what I had done.

A half hour later, I was starting to fall asleep, finally feeling my eyes get heavy, until I was startled awake by my phone.

I grabbed it and looked at the time. It was almost eleven o'clock. Apparently I had slept for nearly four hours, but it felt like I hadn't rested at all.

Antony: Hey

'Hey'? Fucking 'Hey'? That's what he says to me after the day we had, and him disappearing? No.

I tossed the phone back on my nightstand and rolled over. A fresh wave of emotions threatened to make me cry again. A minute later, my phone vibrated once more.

Antony: R u ok? Miguel said you got sick.

Yeah, I got sick, I thought. Sick that I had let myself make such a mistake. Sick when I found out you were a fucking man whore. Sick when I got home and found out my mom had another bad day. Sick when I had to look at my father and pretend like I wasn't a fornicator.

Me: I'm fine.

Antony: Yeah you are ;)

Was he serious? Did he not feel like shit over what we did? Of course not, I realized. It's not the first time he's done this. I had only kissed a few boys, and given head once, but nothing like what we did today.

Me: Thx

**Antony: ur welcome.
Can I call?**

Every part of me was telling me it was a bad idea. I wouldn't be able to control my temper, and I needed to be quiet so my parents wouldn't hear. Granted, my room was the attic, and theirs was on the first floor, but still.

Me: Y

What was the point? If I was just another girl for him, and he's already had me, what was there to talk about. Jesus, I hadn't even made it a challenge for him.

Antony: I just want to hear your voice

The thought of his voice, that perfect, deep, silky sound, both thrilled and disgusted me.

Me: idk. It's been a long day. I guess maybe just for a minute

A second later the phone vibrated with his call.

"Hello," I answered.

"Hey, what's up? You okay?"

"Yeah, I'm fine," I said. I knew it was short and dismissive, but I didn't care.

"Okay good. Miguel said you got sick, and honestly you don't sound fine. You sound like something's wrong."

I sound like something's wrong? I wonder why? Maybe because we just had sex at the convention where we were supposed to be learning about the bible? Nausea hit me again and I didn't respond.

"Is it because of what happened? Do you regret it? Because I don't. You are amazing, and I'm not sorry at all that we gave each other every part of ourselves."

"I'm amazing," I snapped the question. "You don't even know me. Is that what you say to every girl that you've fucked?"

There was a pause on the other side of the line. "Whoa. Um, okay. Well, first off you're the first girl I've 'fucked'," he said, with what sounded like genuine hurt.

"Second, it clearly wasn't your first time, so I don't know why you're mad at me. I know it shouldn't have happened, but I really like you and it just did. Like I said, I'm not sorry, but I get it if you want to forget that it happened. I won't tell anyone, so you don't have to worry about the Elders finding out."

"Not my first time? What the hell is that supposed to mean? I just gave you my fucking virginity and you want to tell me I'm a fucking slut?"

I was furious now, and I knew I needed to be quiet but I wanted to scream at him.

"I never said you were a slut. I just...I don't know."

"What? What the fuck don't you know, Antony?"

"Anything. I don't know anything. Yeah, I've messed around with girls before. I've done oral and stuff, but I've never had sex. And you...you were...," his voice trailed off.

"I was what," I asked, barely controlling my temper.

"Amazing. You were fucking amazing. Like you knew exactly what to do. And you didn't seem like it hurt you. Isn't it supposed to hurt the first time?"

Was he serious? I didn't have a clue what I was doing.

"I didn't know what I was doing, I just...I don't know, I just did what felt good. What felt right in the moment. And no, it didn't hurt. It was a little uncomfortable because you're thicker than my dildo but-"

"Wait, you have toys?"

Shit. I didn't really want anyone to know that. I had ordered one online a few years ago, and was terrified that my parents would find out. But they never asked me about the charge on their card, and I got the package before they could check the mail that day.

"Yeah. I mean no. I…shit," I was stammering, and my anger was slowly slipping from me. "I have *a* toy. A dildo. I like to, you know, play with myself. Don't act like boys don't masturbate all the time."

Another second of silence before he replied. "Yeah, I mean of course. I just thought girls didn't, like I don't know, do that."

I rolled my eyes. "No, girls don't have hormones and urges too. It's strictly for people with a penis."

He laughed, and the last of my anger was gone. "I guess I just never thought about it," he said. "I guess that explains why it didn't hurt. But I'm thicker than your dildo, huh?"

The sound of pride in his voice, and the thought of the way he felt stretching me, made me smile.

"Yeah, I mean I think it's longer, but you definitely, um, you know, stretched me in ways that I had never felt."

Holy shit. There I was again. Saying things I couldn't believe I was saying, not recognizing myself. I tried to feel the guilt that had swept me earlier, but it was gone.

"Hmmm," he said. "Is it there by you now?"

7

The question sent an instant rush of heat between my legs. "Yeah, it's here. Always hidden, but always close."

"When was the last time you used it?"

I smiled. "Last night."

"That was so long ago," he said. I could hear the smile in his voice. "What did you think about?"

Somewhere in the back of my mind a voice was telling me to stop. Hang up, don't do this, it's not right. Fuck that voice.

"I was watching a video on my computer. The guy had the girl bent over the side of his bed, and I imagined it was me."

His voice was lower, even more sexy than normal, when he spoke.

"What was he doing to her?"

I slipped my hand between my legs and began touching myself. "He was spanking her. In perfect rhythm to his thrusts. Every time he buried his cock in her, he smacked her again."

He moaned softly. "I bet your ass would bounce perfectly. Me behind you, thrusting deep inside, one hand smacking your ass, the other one with a fist full of your hair."

I slipped a finger inside of myself. "Oh, fuck that sounds amazing. Me gripping the sheets as you slam in and out, feeling my pussy clench around you."

"I'd have to slow down before I come. Bury it deep inside you, then pull you up and turn your head so I could kiss you."

A second finger. "I'd wrap my arm around your neck and tell you to cum deep inside of me."

"I would do exactly what you said, bringing my hand down to your clit and rubbing it as I come."

I pulled my fingers out and began rubbing, imagining it was his hand on me.

"I'd hold on to you as I felt you explode inside of me. I wouldn't let go until you gave me every drop, then I'd lay you down and suck what was left dry."

"Fuck, you're going to make me come just thinking about it. I'm so hard. Are you using your toy?"

I smiled. "Not yet."

"God, I want you again. I wish I was there right now. I want to taste you."

I wanted that more than he would ever know. An hour ago, I was wracked with guilt, mad at him, and feeling absolutely worthless. Now I felt powerful, sexy, and desperate for his touch.

"I want you to. I want to feel your hands on me again, your mouth, hear your voice whisper in my ear, feel your breath on my neck."

"You know, I could skip the convention tomorrow. We could make this a reality."

A thrill ran through me at the thought, and I shivered. "How?"

"I could come pick you up."

"Yeah, I'm sure my parents would totally go for that," I laughed.

"Well, I have the hotel room until Monday. You could tell your parents that you're going to the convention and come here instead. Do you have your license?"

There it was again, that little voice telling me to stop. We didn't even know each other, and we were talking about getting together and spending the day in his hotel room.

The voice was small, and quickly drowned out by my desire to feel him again.

"Yeah, I've got my license. I'll wait until after Rebecca and her mom leave, and then I'll tell my dad I'm feeling better, and I don't want to miss the program."

"Good. If we wait until after the session starts for the day, you should be able to come up without the risk of anyone seeing you."

My heart raced at the prospect of the day in his bed, and the risk involved. There was a chance that Rebecca's mom would tell my parents that she hadn't seen me at the convention, but as preoccupied as they were right now, I doubted that they would even be talking to her. The thought of my mom brought my mood down a little.

"That sounds amazing," I said, but even to my own ears it sounded weak.

"I'm sorry. If you don't want to, it's okay. I'm not trying to pressure you or anything, it's totally cool if you don't want to come."

He mistook my mood change to be somehow related to our plan. "It's not that," I said. "I just thought about how Rebecca's mom could possibly tell my parents she didn't see me there, but how that probably wouldn't happen because my parents barely talk to anyone anymore."

He sounded relieved that it wasn't about him. "Because of her sickness?"

"Yeah."

"I'm really sorry. I know a little bit of what it's like to watch a family member get sick. Miguel said your mom had been ill, but he didn't say what it was."

"Probably because we don't know. She had some more tests done last week, and they hope the doctors will have some answers on Monday."

"I'm sorry. Look, if you want to stay home and spend the day with your parents, I totally get it."

That would be a disappointment to both of us. "No, it's depressing here. Besides," my smile returning, "I'm going to spend the day naked with you."

I could hear the smile in his voice at his next words. "Now, about that dildo…"

8

    I could barely sleep that night. I tossed and turned after hanging up the phone with Antony. We had talked for another few minutes after we decided that I would come see him, but I was exhausted and tried to sleep. I failed.

    The last time I had looked at the clock was 3:02 in the morning, and then suddenly I was opening my eyes and sunlight was peaking through my blinds. Shit, what time was it?

    I picked up my phone to check the time. I sat straight up in bed. It was almost nine o'clock. My phone showed one missed call from Antony, and four text messages.

Antony: Good morning beautiful

Antony: Do I still get to see you today :)

Antony: Are you okay?

Antony: I'll try giving you a call.

Shit. I hoped he didn't think I was blowing him off. I definitely wanted to spend the day in his arms.

Me: Sorry, just woke up. Gonna jump in the shower and get dressed.

I hopped out of bed and turned my shower on before I jogged down the stairs and into the kitchen. My mom was sitting at the table, an untouched bagel and coffee in front of her.

"Good morning," I said, giving her a quick kiss on the cheek.

She smiled weakly at me. "Good morning, sweetheart. How are you doing? Your dad said you weren't feeling well last night."

I grabbed a bowl out of the cupboard and filled it with cereal. "I'm feeling better. I think I just got overheated yesterday. I was actually thinking if you guys didn't mind, I would take the car and just drive myself to the convention."

"Oh. I guess that would be okay, but you have to check with your dad. He ran to get more bread; he'll be back soon."

I sat down across from her with my breakfast. I stopped and looked at her for the first time this morning, and my heart sank.

A year ago, she was the most active person I knew. Always spending time with me in the door-to-door ministry, taking care of her garden, helping sick and older people in the congregation.

Now she was the sick one. Her face looked gaunt, and her hands were almost skeletal, her skin stretched thin and translucent over her body.

"Mom," I started, but had to pause to swallow back the lump in my throat. "I can always just stay home with you. We could watch a movie or something."

She smiled and shook her head. "No, you go hunny. I am going to try to rest and listen to yesterday's program. Nancy dropped off the tapes before her and Rebecca headed there this morning."

Guilt pricked at the back of my mind. My mother wished nothing more than to be in attendance at the convention, and here I was perfectly able to go but going to skip to go do things that I knew were wrong.

But those 'wrong' things made me feel so good, and the guilt was washed away by the thrill that the idea of his hands on my body again brought.

"Okay," I said with a shrug. "If you're sure."

She reached out and patted my hand. "Of course."

I finished my cereal quickly, rinsing out my bowl and putting it in the dishwasher.

"I'm going to jump in the shower. Can you ask dad if I can take the car when he gets home?"

My mother just nodded. She looked so weak, such a shell of the woman she once was.

I ran up the stairs, two at a time, and jumped in the shower. I had planned on taking a quick shower. That changed when I thought again about the opportunity to spend the day with Antony. We could take our time, be as loud as we wanted, do whatever we wanted as many *times* as we wanted.

I slid one hand over my breast and teased my nipple, as my other hand went down, slipping between my wet lips.

I thought about the way his hand had felt touching me, his fingers sliding in and out of me with ease. I wished I had a bigger shower, one with a tub attached, but my attic shower was little more than a box with a nozzle.

I slipped a finger inside myself and started rubbing my clit with my palm. The memory of Antony's fingers touching my most private spot drove me closer to an orgasam.

As I thought about all of the things that we would do today, I felt myself go over the edge. I rubbed myself automatically, my hand moving on pure reflex as I came. I heard a knock, and my hand stopped.

"Just a minute," I said breathlessly.

Shit, had I been moaning? I was usually so careful not to make noise, but since Antony everything was more intense, and I could feel myself darken with embarrassment. I wrapped a towel around myself and opened the bathroom door. My mom sat on the bed.

"Mom, what are you doing? You shouldn't have climbed the stairs, you should have just called me and I would've come down to you."

She smiled weakly. "I'm not an invalid, I can still climb the stairs," she sighed. "Probably sooner than later I won't be able to, but until then I'll do what I can. But that's not why I came up here."

I took the towel off and began drying my hair. "What's up," I asked through the towel.

"Your dad had to leave, something came up at work and he's going to be gone for a couple of hours. But he left the keys to my car, so you can take that."

She looked so weak. "Mom, are you going to be okay if I go," I asked, wrapping the towel back around me. I can skip, or wait until he gets home and catch the afternoon program."

My mom just smiled at me. "No, baby, you go. I'll be fine. I'm just going to lay in bed and listen to yesterday's talks."

I gave her a quick hug. "Okay, well if you need me just call or text me."

"You know I hate that text messaging stuff."

I just smiled and she went back downstairs.

I dropped my towel and looked in the mirror. My curves were as soft as ever, my ample C cup breasts perky, nipple hard against the cool air of my room.

I imagined Antony teasing them with his mouth, and I was instantly wet again. My hand running down my stomach, past my shaved mound, and in between my lips.

I wanted to make myself come right then, but I knew it wouldn't be anything compared to what he would do to me. So instead, I went to my drawer and looked through my underwear.

I picked a pink lacy thong. I was about to grab a bra, but decided against it at the last minute. I could easily sneak past my mom without her knowing I wasn't wearing one, and the look on Antony's face when he took my top off and saw nothing under it would be irresistible.

A few moments later, I was dressed in a long skirt that hugged my curves, one that my mom always said was 'too tight on my booty', and a loose top. I put a shawl over it, and skipped down the stairs.

"You're sure you will be okay alone," I asked my mom as I gave her a quick hug.

"I'll be fine. Go learn, I love to see you taking your relationship with Jehovah seriously."

There was that quick pang of guilt again, but it was just as quickly overruled by my desire.

"Okay. I'll call when I'm on my way back. Might go out to eat after the program," I said as I closed the door and made my way to the car.

Five minutes later I was on the interstate, headed to Cleveland. Just not the place in Cleveland that my parents thought. As I drove, I thought about all of the things we would be doing in his hotel room.

9

As I got off of the highway, I texted Antony.

Be there in 10. Where should I meet you?

His response was instant. He must have been waiting for me to message him. I pictured him in his bed, touching himself while he thought about me coming to see him.

Antony: Meet you in lobby.

As I parked the car, a moment of guilt came over me again. I should probably pray for strength to turn around right now and go home and tell my parents exactly what I did yesterday.

Except that that would crush them, and I would probably be disfellowshipped; at the very least I would be publicly reproved and lose all of my privileges. Everyone would gossip and talk about me, and my reputation would never be the same.

Plus, deep down, I wanted this. I loved the power I felt when I took Antony inside of me; I had spent so much time being the 'good girl', and in the end I had barely any real friends, my mom was sick, and no matter how much I prayed things weren't getting better.

No, I would enjoy every moment of this day. I walked into the hotel and found that he was already there in the lobby waiting for me. He looked amazing in his jeans and tight tee shirt.

It dawned on me then that he had seen most of me, but neither of us had been fully naked. And we had been in a cramped car.

Would he still like what he saw when he had room to take me in? I pushed down my insecurities about not having the perfect thin body that guys all seemed to like.

"Hey," he said, his voice causing an immediate reaction in me.

"Hi," I said as I went to give him a hug. It was awkward at best, and left me even more nervous.

Shit, what if this was a mistake? What if we were only going to have the moments we had, and nothing more?

If he was nervous, he didn't show it. "Come on, the elevator is this way."

He let me go in the elevator first, and he hit the button for the second floor. And the third. And the fourth. All the way up to seven.

"Did you forget what floor you were on," I asked playfully.

"No," he said as the door shut. "I just wanted more time to do this."

He grabbed my hips and spun my back to the wall. I let out a squeal of shock and delight and wrapped my arms around his neck as his lips found mine.

There was no hesitation in his kiss, and I took it in eagerly. His hand roaming to my breast just as the 'ding' sounded and the door opened for the second floor.

He was off of me in an instant, standing there like we were just strangers. When no one was there and the door closed, his attention was right back to me. The rest of the elevator ride we didn't stop for the 'ding'.

If anyone had been there when the doors opened, they would have found us fully enveloped in each other's bodies.

"This way," he said when we finally reached the seventh floor.

He took my hand and we practically ran down the hallway. He swiped his card, the 'Do Not Disturb' marker already hanging from the door handle.

He pulled me to the bed and kissed me. I would have stood there kissing him for hours, but he pushed me down onto the bed.

"You're gorgeous," he said breathlessly, taking in my clothed curves.

"I'm even better without this on," I smiled, gesturing the length of my body.

He smiled in a way I hadn't seen him do. "Show me."

I wasn't prepared for that. I pictured him ripping my clothes off, not me stripping for him. I didn't hesitate though.

That voice, and the power in his command, had me pulling my top over my head. I laid back down, my breasts fully exposed for him to see.

"Fuck," was all he said as I slipped out of my skirt.

When I was in just my thong, he came to the edge of the bed and rolled me over. I gasped as he took my ass in his hands and spread my cheeks.

I knew that my thong wouldn't cover much from that angle, and the thought of him seeing me so exposed drove me wild.

I felt his finger slide under my thong, and his knuckle brushed against my asshole. I pushed my hips up.

"You look delicious."

Before I could respond, he wrapped his arms under my hips and pulled my ass up fully. His tongue brushed my clit before slowly going up the length of my wet slit.

But he didn't stop. I inhaled sharply as his tongue pushed against my forbidden hole.

"Oh my god, what are-". I didn't finish the question as his tongue pushed deeper inside. The sensation was like a shot of fire through my body and I moaned.

He rolled me over and pinned my legs back, his face on it's way to being buried between my legs again. I had showered this morning before I came over, but…my thoughts were once again taken from me as his tongue teased my ass.

I gave in and relaxed, my body pushing all rational thought from my mind. I grabbed the back of his head and pushed gently against his eager mouth. I was rewarded with a moan from him, and the feeling of a finger being slipped inside of my wet and eager body.

I ran my fingers through his curls as I began to undulate faster. He used a second finger and I could feel my orgasm building. The only time his tongue stopped pleasing my body was when I moaned softly.

"You don't have to be quiet, I want to hear what I do to you," he said breathily before returning his mouth.

His wish was my command. As I pushed against him and bucked faster, he used his free hand to pull me to him. I clenched the sheets and moaned. I felt myself coming, and I knew he was going to be soaked but I didn't care. As my orgasm slowed, I started to pull away.

"No, not yet," he said, as he wrapped both of his arms around my thighs and pulled my clit to his mouth. I screamed with pleasure as I came a second time, more intensely than I ever had before.

He pulled his mouth back, but didn't remove it from between my thighs. The smile on his face was intoxicating.

"I…that was…I've never gone a second time so fast like that," I stuttered and stumbled.

He licked his lips and went right back to teasing me.

"Oh my god, again," I asked.

"Mhmm," he mumbled without removing his lips from mine and the vibration thrilled me.

I rode the wave over and over, before I finally pushed him back. I wanted more so bad, I had never felt like this before, but I needed a break.

He slipped next to me in the bed, and I felt his length against me. I rolled on my side to face him.

"You enjoyed that," I asked, rubbing my hand over the outline of his bulge.

I had only had one other boy give me oral, and he stopped after less than a minute, asking me if I had cum. I was shocked when a week later a bunch of the kids in my school were talking about how he had 'suffered through my terrible taste' and made me come over and over again.

"God yes," he said, running his finger gently up and down my exposed body. "You taste amazing."

"I…I didn't think boys enjoyed doing that."

He smiled. "Boys might not, but I'm a man."

I was going to make a joke of some sort, but before I could speak his mouth was on mine. I parted my lips and kissed him deeply. He was right, I did taste amazing.

I tried to undo his jeans while we kissed, and failed miserably.

"Would you like me to help with that," he asked with that smile that I was coming to crave.

I was sure I blushed, but I just nodded.

He stood and unbuttoned his jeans, pulling them down but leaving his boxer briefs clinging to the outline of him.

The muscles of his legs were clearly defined, and I tried to figure out how I had missed that before. I guess we had just been rushed and half-dressed when we were with each other yesterday.

God, had it really been only one day? One day and I was fully engrossed in this man that I barely knew.

He started to get back in bed with his underwear and tee shirt still on. "Uh-uh, all of it," I said, circling the air with my finger.

He smiled and obliged. He took his boxers off first, his dick catching and then popping up as the cloth slipped down his legs. When he took his shirt off I was thrilled by what I saw.

The only part of him that wasn't tanned was where his boxers sat. The man looked like he spent every day in the gym.

"Shit, you have a perfect body," I said.

"Perks of working at a job that requires me to be in shape, I guess," he said nonchalantly.

Another reminder that I knew very little about him.

"What do you do," I asked as he lay back down beside me and pulled me close.

"You," practically whispered.

His voice and our naked bodies lying next to each other made me wet again. I almost couldn't focus. Almost.

"No, but really," I said, smacking him playfully on the arm, "what do you do? I don't know anything about you."

He pulled himself back just a little bit to look at me, and I instantly regretted asking him the question. I wanted his body on mine, inside of mine.

"I do landscaping. It's not much right now, but I think in the next year or two I should be able to start my own company."

That explained his perfect tan. "That's so cool," I said genuinely.

He laughed. "Oh yeah, manual labor for shit pay is awesome."

I took his hand. "No, I mean it. The fact that you are going to start your own business. That's cool. And," I said, moving his hand down my stomach and between my legs, "you certainly know how to use your hands."

10

The lust in his eyes as he plunged his fingers into me made me mad with desire. I loved the way it felt when he made me come, but I wanted to do things to him.

"It's my turn," I said, slipping away from his touch. "Lay down."

He did as I instructed, and I looked him up and down. Yesterday I had thought him to be a bit nerdy, and just average to look at.

But now, seeing his perfect body laying here, his cock hard like his muscles, I couldn't help but think I was so very wrong.

I must have stared just a moment too long. "What," he asked, looking shy.

"I was just enjoying the view," I said with a smile as I moved my hands up his body.

I rubbed his strong calves, up to his thighs, I took him in one hand as the other gently squeezed his balls. His back arched and he let out a small gasp.

"Do you like the way my hands feel?"

He just nodded. I moved my hands further up, across his rippled stomach, slowly across his chest pinching both of his nipples. I took his face in my hands.

"Do you like the way my pussy feels," I asked as I slid his hard shaft up and down between my wet lips.

"Fuck yes," he said with a smile.

"You make me so wet," I said as I continue to grind on him. "I bet you would slip right in. Is that what you want? Do you want to feel your cock inside of me again?"

He didn't answer. Instead, he rolled me over in a flash. His hands gripped the inside of my thighs as he spread my legs wide. Slowly, gently, he slid the head of his dick inside of me. I wanted it all, and I tried to push against him, but he held me down.

"Be patient," he said.

In and out, he slowly put a little more of himself inside of me with each deliberate movement.

"I need all of you," I practically begged.

"Oh yeah,' he asked, and drove his full length inside of me.

I screamed out in pleasure as he did it again, a little bit faster. Soon his hips were slamming into mine, hard and fast. I wrapped my hand around the back of his neck and gripped the sheets with my other.

"Fuck me, fuck me, don't stop," I cried out as I began lifting my hips in time with his thrusts.

"Oh fuck," he said in between breathes. "Fuck, I'm going to come."

I pulled his face down to mine. "No," I whispered with a smile before I pushed him from me.

The look on his face was a mix of disappointment and desire as I pushed him down to where I had been laying.

"You're going to come in my mouth first," I said, swinging my ass into his face and taking all of him into my mouth.

I was rewarded with his hands on my bottom as he spread my cheeks. His tongue was on my clit in an instant, and I pushed back against his face in sync with my mouth milking his cock. I felt his fingers go in closer to my forbidden sweet spot. Oh fuck. Fuck we're doing this again.

His tongue moved from one hole to the other, rimming me teasingly, and I moaned on his cock.

"Do you like the way my tongue feels," he asked.

I pulled him from my mouth for just a moment. "Do you like the way my ass tastes?"

"Fuck yes," he said as he stuck his tongue back in as far as he could.

I gripped his cock with my hand and moaned. I used my hand to rub him as he shoved his tongue in and out of my forbidden hole.

A finger slipped inside of my pussy and I lost all conscious thought. I began pushing against his face in rhythm with his fingers and tongue.

"Fuck, you're going to make me come again," I said as I fucked his face.

Suddenly he pulled his finger and tongue out of me. I thought he was going to tell me no like I had done to him.

Instead, I felt his finger slip inside of my ass as his tongue found its way back to my clit. I screamed as the wave of the orgasm ripped over me.

And then…I farted.

11

Oh. My. God. To say that I was mortified would be the understatement of the millennium. And that was before he started laughing.

I was off of him in an instant, running to the bathroom and locking myself in. I had never been so embarrassed in my life.

I thought about the boy in school that had said I tasted terrible and the embarrassment that I had felt then. I had played sick for almost a week before my mother had demanded that I go to the doctor. I went back to school instead. That was nothing compared to this.

I felt tears on my cheeks before I even realized that I was crying. I grabbed some tissue and wiped them away furiously as he knocked gently on the door.

"Em, open up, it's okay."

No the fuck it was not okay.

He waited a second before knocking again.

"Go away," I said. I would stay locked in here all day if I had to.

"Babe, please, come on, it's okay. Just let me in."

'Babe'? I practically shit on his face, and he decided that *this* was the moment to call me 'babe'?

He might have been right though, because it worked. I unlocked the door and sat down on the edge of the shower.

"Are you okay," he asked as he opened the door slowly.

What a dumb question. I am not even close to okay. I looked down, trying to hide the tears, but he knelt in front of me and lifted my chin. I tried not to notice his still semi-hardness as my eyes went to his.

"Why are you crying," he asked, wiping my tears away.

Another dumb question, and I started to answer, but my voice failed me, and I sobbed instead.

He pulled me into him and held me. "Really, it's not that big of a deal. It's okay, I promise," he said quietly as I sobbed in his arms.

"Until you tell all of your friends how I shit on your face," I choked out between sobs.

He pulled back and looked at me. "I would never tell anyone. What we do is between us. Jesus, is that what you think of me?"

As he stood and started to back away, I realized he had no way to know what memories this had triggered. No way to know the embarrassment of what I had just done.

"I'm sorry, I just," I tried to speak, but the look on his face was one of pure hurt at my words.

"I'm sorry," I said again.

"It's okay," he said, but I could tell that my words had hurt him.

"It's not, and I'm sorry. You're right, it wasn't fair to you to say what I said, and I guess I'm just embarrassed," I said lowering my head again.

He sighed. "You have nothing to be embarrassed for. But, if it'll make you feel better, I could fart next time you're sucking me."

I looked up at him and smiled. "Um, first, no. Second, what makes you think there will be a next time?"

He smiled back and gestured down his body. "Can you really resist this?"

I looked at his again growing size. "No," I said as I took his half hard cock in my mouth and sucked it once, letting it fall out with a distinct 'pop'.

"Good. Then, how about we go back to the bed," he said when I drew my face back from him.

I stood. "Or we could take a shower and get something to eat," I said as I turned and began running the water.

I felt him behind me in an instant, his hard dick sliding between my legs. I let out a breath and closed my eyes reaching back and bringing his lips to my neck.

As he kissed, his hands roamed my body slowly. It took every ounce of self-control that I had to pull away from him and step into the shower.

I looked back at him, his gaze hungrily moving up and down my now wet body. "Are you coming?"

He smiled as he stepped into the shower. "I hope we both are."

I had touched myself so many times in the shower, the one place where I could be just a little bit loud and expect the water to drown out the sound. How many times had I imagined a man with me, kissing me, touching me?

As if reading my mind, he pulled close to me, kissing me as he pinned my back to the shower wall.

"I want you," he said in a sultry whisper.

I pushed him back from me and dropped to my knees, water cascading down my long hair and off my back. He gasped as I took his stiff length into my mouth and began sucking him eagerly.

I didn't stop him when he grabbed a hand full of my wet hair. I tried to match his rhythm as he began thrusting into my mouth, but soon I gave him full control. The feeling of him using my mouth for his pleasure drove me wild, and if he hadn't come when he did, I might have.

"Oh shit," I heard him say as his cock started to twitch.

One more full thrust and he held it in my throat. I swallowed as he released into me. When he finished, I stood and kissed him.

I expected him to resist, but he kissed me long and deep, and the rush of knowing he was tasting himself on my kiss drove me wild.

"Take me," I said as I turned and grabbed onto the shower bar.

I moaned out as his still hard cock went all of the way inside of me with his first thrust. My moan seemed to drive him, and he began pumping faster and faster.

It hadn't even been two days, but I knew that I wanted this man inside of me forever. I didn't want another's touch. I wanted *his* fingers, *his* tongue, *his* cock.

He started to slow, his thrusts not going as deep. "What's wrong," I asked.

"Nothing, I just, I didn't get condoms. I should've. We shouldn't do this without protection."

I turned my head to look at him. The look in his eyes was maddening. He wanted me as bad as I wanted him.

"It's fine, I'm on birth control," I said. "Now fuck me until you come."

He needed no further encouragement. Soon, his hips were slamming into my backside again, one of his hands on the shower wall, the other on my shoulder.

"Fuck, fuck you feel so fucking perfect," he said as he continued to drive himself in and out of me.

"Don't stop," I begged, "let me feel you come."

He did, not stopping for another ten minutes before he pushed in and held himself there, putting both hands on my shoulders and moaning deeply.

Yes, yes, that was what I wanted to feel. He pulled out, and I turned to him.

"Now we can get clean and get something to eat."

He watched as I washed my body. I tried to be as sexy as I could soaping myself up, but I had no idea if it was working. Until his dick started to get hard again.

"Um, again" I asked, pointing.

He smiled. "You have that effect on me."

"Feel the effect you have on me," I said as I took his hand and put it on my slick heat.

He slid a finger in. When I moaned, he added another. By the time we left the shower, we had both come more than once.

12

Antony had gotten out of the shower before me, and when I stepped out of the bathroom wrapped in a towel he was already dressed in his jeans and tee shirt.

My first thought was of how badly I wanted to pull them off of him. My second was the realization that I had only the skirt and top that I had worn when I left my house this morning.

"Crap," I said, slumping my shoulders.

"I look that bad?"

The playful smirk on his face made me smile.

"No, I just don't have casual clothes," I said gesturing to the pile where my skirt lay.

"Oh. Well," he said as he pulled his shirt over his head, "I'll just throw on slacks and a button down."

His abs made me pause. He caught me looking and smiled.

"You know, it's not fair that I have no shirt on," he said, closing the distance between us in two strides and hooking his finger under the lip of my towel between my breasts, "and yet you are covered."

I pulled back, knowing that his hold on my towel would make if fall from my body.

"Is that better," I asked, smiling as he eyed up and down my still damp body.

"Fuck yes."

He kissed me, and when I felt his hand start to go from my cheek to my breast, I pushed him.

"Stop," I said with a little giggle. "I need fuel or we won't be able to have any more fun."

He gave an exaggerated pout and began dressing. I couldn't help but notice his eyes on me as I sat on the bed and started to pull my underwear on. I smiled at his sigh when I lifted my hips and spread my knees.

"You're the one that wanted fuel," he mumbled.

A few minutes later we were walking out of the hotel, hand in hand, headed toward East 4th Street. The food smelled amazing, and I was absolutely starving. He picked an Italian place and I couldn't wait to get my mouth on some pasta.

"Should we eat here, or get it to go," he asked as we approached the door.

I shrugged. "I guess I assumed we would sit down and eat."

"Why not," he said as he pulled the door open and asked for a table for two.

We were shown to a table, and he pulled the chair out for me. My heart gave a little flutter.

"Thank you."

"You're welcome," he said, and his low reply had me wishing that we had gotten the food to go. The sooner we were naked again the better.

We had gotten through the incredible antipasto that he had ordered as an appetizer when he reached across and held my hand. We sat there, talking and laughing between bites of our entrees.

"Dessert," he asked, as he dabbed his mouth with a napkin.

"I can think of something I'd like in my mouth for dessert," I said with a terrible attempt at a wink.

He laughed. "That wink was terrifying, but I do like where you were going with that. You should get some cannoli, it's phenomenal!"

"It was not, terrifying" I said as I playfully slapped his arm. "I'm stuffed. But you can get something if you want."

When the waiter returned, Antony ordered his cannoli. When it arrived, I instantly regretted not ordering one because it looked to die for.

As he ate it, he must have noticed my longing looks towards it.

"Here," he said, and cut off a piece.

I leaned forward and ate it from his fork. I'm pretty sure the moan that I gave rivaled some that he had heard me make earlier.

"That good," he asked with a smile. "I told you that you should've gotten some."

I just smiled and finished chewing.

"Oh, you've got a little..." he reached across and wiped some of the cream from my lip.

I pulled his finger into my mouth and sucked on it for just a split second. His smile told me he wanted me to suck on more than his finger.

But his smile fell, and he quickly pulled his finger back, just as I heard a voice from behind me.

"Brother Householder."

I cringed. Fuck. Fuck, fuck, fuck. I didn't recognize the voice, but as he came into my line of sight, I'm sure I looked like I had just been caught blowing Antony.

"Sister Marquette," Brother Jackson said with a smile that made me want to cry.

"Brother Jackson, I…we…how are you," Antony said, reaching out to shake his hand.

Brother Jackson just looked at the hand that Antony extended. "I'm well, but I think I'll refrain from shaking your hand just now."

Oh my god. He had seen me sucking Antony's finger. Jesus fucking Christ. I was dead. I was done for. My parents would kill me, and I would wake up in the New System.

Antony turned about six shades darker and quickly pulled his hand back. Brother Jackson just patted him on the shoulder.

"Glad to see you're feeling better," he said as he walked away.

Antony quickly called the waiter over and gave him cash. "Keep the change," he said as we practically ran from the restaurant.

When we got to the street, he started to laugh. I was nearly in tears, and he started to laugh.

"What the fuck is wrong with you," I snapped. "We're going to be in serious fucking trouble. At the very least, we're going to be pulled into the back room."

He sobered. "For what? Having lunch? I promise, it will be okay."

I turned away from him. I was going to cry, and I didn't want him to see my tears.

"No, it's not. I've never been in trouble with the Elders. They don't know I curse, they definitely don't know about the boys that I messed around with in school, and they absolutely do not know that we are fucking."

He didn't try to look at me. "What boys? And we're just 'fucking'?"

I couldn't tell what emotion I heard in his voice. Pain? Sadness? Shock? Confusion? Jealousy? I didn't know, but I didn't like it.

Fuck. Five minutes ago we were having an amazing day. Now, we were ruined. I didn't answer.

"Let's just get back to the hotel, everything will be fine."

13

When we got back to the room, I sat in the small chair that all hotels have; they're never comfortable, but I didn't notice.

I was on the verge of crying. "How long do you think until we get called into the back room?"

Antony sat on the edge of the bed with a sigh. "I don't know. Hell, I don't even know if we will."

My eyes shot to his, my almost tears bursting into full tears of anger.

"Are you kidding? You told them you were sick. I told my parents I was going to go to the convention. We were seen eating together, without a chaperone, and I was sucking on your damn finger."

He came over to me and knelt in front of me. "Okay. So, here's the story. You went to the convention, but didn't sit with Rebecca and her family. At lunch, you were hungry and realized that you hadn't packed anything."

The idea of lying to my parents even more made me sick. Not because of the actual act of the lie, I could live with that.

No, it was the fact that the more a person lies, the more likely that it is that they will be caught in that lie. His story made sense so far.

"Okay. I texted Becca, but she didn't answer. So, I texted you to see if you were around her or Miguel. You weren't because you were sick, but you said you needed to eat anyway so I met you at the restaurant. We had lunch in a crowd full of people, we were never alone," I picked up the storyline, extending it.

Antony nodded. "Yeah, yeah that's good. The Elder's will complain that we didn't have a chaperone, but if you haven't been in trouble like this before," he trailed off raising an eyebrow.

I shook my head, and he continued.

"Then they will probably just tell you to make sure that you are more careful, and remind you that everything you do reflects on Jehovah, etcetera, etcetera, etcetera. And we'll just tell them that Brother Jackson was mistaken at what he thought he saw."

I nodded. My anger, and fear of the Elders was waning.

"Okay, that might work. I'll have to text Becca and make sure she'll cover. I'm sure she will. Do you think I should go to the afternoon session?"

Antony shrugged. "You could. Or you could stay here, and we could spend a few more hours together."

I scrunched up my nose. "Don't you think if no one sees me they'll know I wasn't there?"

"Nah, there's got to be at least 6,000 people there today. I'm sure it'll be fine."

I smiled as I texted Becca. "This might just work."

Me: Hey. If ANYONE asks I need you to tell them I texted you at lunch time today but you didn't see it.

As I clutched the phone waiting for Becca's reply, Antony cleared his throat. He had sat back down on the bed.

"So, umm," he said, running a hand through his perfect hair, "about earlier. You've been with other guys?"

I cringed, thinking about how I had brushed off the earlier comment.

"I mean, you've been with other girls."

He chuckled nervously. "Yeah, but, just like some kissing and touching and stuff."

I felt myself flush with embarrassment. "I may have, back in high school, given a guy head. And he may have returned the favor."

I couldn't tell the look on his face. "But you never slept with them?"

I came over to where he sat on the bed and straddled him. "No, I told you I was a virgin until you."

"Until we began 'fucking'," he asked, his eyes clearly hungry.

I brought my lips to his ear. "Until your hard cock went inside my wet pussy," I whispered.

I felt his lips on my neck, down to my collar bone. His hands went under my shirt and pulled it off.

"Maybe you should remind me of what that's like," his perfect voice said.

The next hour and a half flew by. The look in his eye when he fucked me.

No, he didn't fuck me. When he made love to me, made me feel like I was his Queen. He laid down next to me in bed and pulled me close to him, my back pressed tight to his strong chest as his arms wrapped around me.

"I was thinking that we should try actually dating. Like, you know, we're supposed to. In a group, with other people from the Kingdom Hall around," he said, as his finger ran up and down my belly.

I turned to look at him. "You want people to know about us?"

He smiled, but then it faded. "Yeah, but if you don't want to-"

I cut him off. "Of course, yes."

He kissed me deeply, and I curled into him. I hadn't had a boyfriend before, and it was funny to think about the idea. I fell asleep imagining what it would be like to go out in public and not have to hide holding his hand.

14

When I woke up, Antony was breathing softly with his arm still over me. I smiled and looked at him in the orange hue of the late sun coming through the window. Oh shit!

I jumped up. "Oh my god, what time is it," I said, waking him up as I scrambled for my phone.

My phone said that it was 8:34. Holy shit, I should've been home at least two hours ago. It was worse when I saw all of the missed texts and calls. Four calls from my parents. And texts from them and Becca.

Becca: Of course I'll cover. What am I covering for?

You there?

Girl, it's been four hours since you texted me whats up

Mom: Are you okay?

Becca: Your mom called. Where are you? I'm starting to worry.

Holy fuck. I was screwed. Antony was over my shoulder.

"It'll be fine. Let me see your phone."

I handed him the phone and he typed a few messages and gave it back.

"It'll be fine," he repeated. "Get dressed and I'll walk you out."

As he gave me a kiss on the head, I looked at what he sent.

Me to Becca: Sorry, battery died. I'll give you details soon.

Me to Mom: Sorry, battery died. Went out to eat with some friends after the convention. Just got back to the car after dinner, charging my phone and heading home now. See you soon.

I felt a twinge of guilt at the lies, but if I was being honest, both should work perfectly. Sure, my parents will be upset that I didn't call them to let them know I was going out to eat before I did.

But I'll just tell them I was going to let them know when I got to the restaurant, but my battery died before I could call them.

And Becca I would give some details to. Some.

Becca: I want the details as soon as you can call. Where r u?

Me: About to be omw home. I'll call you in like an hour.

I pulled my clothes on. "I got to go," I said, giving Antony a quick kiss. "I'll let you know when I get home."

"I'll walk you out," he said, pulling on his shoes.

I shook my head. "No, the program is over and there might be other Witnesses here. I don't want to risk them seeing you and me at a hotel."

He gave me another kiss, and I walked out the door. When I got in the elevator and the doors closed, my heart started to race.

I was worried about what my parents would say when I got home. I was nervous about what would come of Brother Jackson having seen us at lunch. I was still giddy about the idea of dating Antony.

When I finally got out of the elevator, I realized that one thing I wasn't feeling was the guilt or shame that I had started to feel yesterday.

Sure, I knew that what we were doing was considered wrong, that I should feel guilty for it. But it didn't feel wrong; it felt beautiful. I was smiling when I got into the driver seat of my moms car and drove home.

Before I parked went into my house, I grabbed my phone.

Me: Just got home. I'll call you as soon as my parents are done murdering me :'(

I unlocked the door and took a breath. When I pushed the door open and went inside my dad was sitting in his chair. No book, the TV wasn't on, just sitting there looking at me.

"I'm sorry, my-"

"Battery died," he cut me off. "Yeah, we finally got your text. Your mom should have been in bed hours ago, but she insisted on staying up to make sure you were okay. What the heck were you thinking? She was worried sick, and she has her doctor's appointment tomorrow morning. She needs her rest. And you need to be more considerate."

He didn't yell. He didn't curse. He had never been one for spanking when I was little. But his words hit me like a punch.

"I'm sorry."

"Apologize to your mother in the morning, she finally had to go to bed. I've got to work tomorrow, so you'll need to take her to her appointment."

I just nodded and went up to my attic. I didn't mind that I would have to take my mom, it was the least I could do.

I was feeling guilt finally, but it wasn't over the things that me and Antony had done. It was over the fact that I added stress to my already over stressed parents.

Me: I made it. Thank you for a great day, I'm going to go to bed.

I tossed the phone down and undressed. I decided to take a shower tonight, so that in the morning I wouldn't have to worry about it before we had to leave for the doctor.

Antony: You're welcome, I enjoyed it too. You going to call?

I wanted to. God did I want to hear his voice.

Me: No, I gotta take a shower and get to sleep. Taking mom to doctor tomorrow.

I started the shower before walking back into my bedroom and looking in the mirror. I wasn't a conceited person, my whole life I'd been called fat or chubby by guys. My curves were strong, my breasts full and perky. I turned and looked at my ass.

Yep, that was definitely impossible to hide no matter how baggy of clothes I tried to hide it in. I had always been taught that I should hide my body, be ashamed of it, lest I make someone in the Kingdom Hall stumble. But Antony's gaze had given me a confidence that made my pride soar.

How is it my job to hide myself just because some Brothers can't keep their eyes to themselves? My phone vibrated, pulling me from my thoughts.

Antony: Ok. I'm here if you change your mind. I hope you sleep well :*

Me: :*

I showered quickly and climbed into bed. I fell asleep wishing that I was sleeping in Antony's arms again.

15

I woke up to the sound of the alarm going off on my phone. When I reached over to silence it, I almost squealed at the text that was on it.

Antony: Hey, I know you're probably sleeping. I just wanted to say that I am excited at the idea of dating you. I was thinking maybe this weekend we could do something?

I pulled my phone to my chest and smiled. I had a boyfriend! And he was sweet. And he was damn gorgeous. I tossed on jeans and a top and went to grab some breakfast.

"You're up early," my mom said when she saw me come into the kitchen.

Despite her being sick, she was always up before me, sitting at the table drinking her coffee and watching the news.

"I wanted to make sure I was ready to take you to your appointment," I said as I gave her a good morning kiss on the cheek.

"Well thank you for taking me. Your dad would if he could've gotten out of work."

I poured myself a bowl of cereal and sat down across from her.

"I just hope they have some good news."

Mom shrugged. "I don't think there is going to be good news at this point, but I'll settle for just knowing what's wrong with me."

She muted the TV before looking back to me. "Your dad says you went out to eat last night with some friends. Was there a Brother involved?"

I couldn't help but smile. "Maybe."

Mom smiled back. "Well I knew it would happen sooner or later. You just remember to keep putting Jehovah and your ministry first. A good Brother will support you, not be an obstacle. What's his name?"

"Antony," I said, poking at the cereal with my spoon. "And he's pretty amazing. He goes to the Sandusky hall, and he's friends with Miguel."

She reached across the table and put her hand on mine. "Just remember your priorities and go slow. If he's a good Brother, he won't pressure you to do anything that might bring reproach on Jehovah's name."

A split second of guilt washed over me, but it was gone just as quickly. I smiled at her.

"I know mom. When do we need to leave?"

Mom glanced at the clock. "In about a half hour."

I finished my cereal and took my bowl to the sink. "Okay, I'm going to take a shower real quick then."

I ran back upstairs and turned the shower on. Yeah, I had taken one last night. But this wasn't about getting clean.

Me: I'm going to take a shower. Wish you were here to take one with me :P

Antony's response was nearly immediate, and I felt a rush of heat when I read it.

Antony: If I was there, we'd be doing very little showering. But you would definitely be wet.

Me: I already am wet, and I haven't gotten in yet ;)

**Antony: Damn I wish I
could see**

**Me: I do have a digital
camera. What's your email?**

I went to my dresser and pulled
out the camera that I had gotten last
year. I had wanted to be a photographer
for a short time, but I never stuck with it.
I stood in front of the mirror and
smiled. I slid my hand down to cover
myself and took the picture. A few
minutes later I had uploaded it and sent
it to the email he gave me.

Me: Check your email :)

I jumped in the shower, and
imagined he was with me. It didn't take
long to finish, and I was dressed and in
the living room waiting for my mom with
plenty of time to spare.
I heard her coming out of the
hallway from her bedroom, and when I
looked, I nearly cried. She looked so
weak. She looked scared, like today she
might get the worst news of her life.

"Mom," I said, rushing to her side and linking my arm with hers. "Let me help you."

I sat her on the couch.

"Thank you," she said, and I could see now that she had been crying.

"It's going to be okay mom. You'll be okay."

She looked at me and smiled. Her smile was not weak, it was calm and strong.

"I know," she said. "Jehovah will not test us more than we can bear. So whatever this is, he will help me fight through it."

My heart sank. I wanted to scream at her. My anger felt irrational, but I was so mad. How could she say that still? How could she sit there and believe that God would do anything to help her when he hadn't for the last year.

It wasn't Jehovah taking her to her appointments, he wasn't the one cleaning her up when she was sick, he wasn't the one that had been there for her through all of this. It was my father and I.

I tried to smile. I couldn't bring myself to do it though, so I just stood and went into the kitchen.

"I'm going to grab the keys, then we'll head out."

I propped myself up against the sink, and I cried. I shook silently with my tears, tears of anger, frustration, fear. I made sure that she couldn't hear a sound, and then I wiped my eyes and grabbed the keys.

"Tell me more about this boy. Antony? Is he a Ministerial Servant? How old is he? What are his parents like," she asked once we were driving.

I sighed. "He is not a Ministerial Servant, no. But he was an attendant at the convention. He is twenty-six, and I haven't met his parents. I've only just met him," I chuckled.

My mom was not laughing. "Twenty-six and he's not an MS? Is he a pioneer?"

I sighed again, this time a little heavier and I had to fight the urge to roll my eyes.

"No, he's not a pioneer mom. But he's a good brother," I smiled, she probably thought it was because I was thinking about how good he is, but I was definitely thinking about how bad he is, "and Miguel is friends with him, so that's got to count for something, right?"

"Maybe. When do we get to meet him?"

Jesus Christ. I hadn't even officially started dating him yet, and she was talking about meeting parents.

"I don't know. He's busy, he does landscaping and is trying to start his own business."

"Well, I hope he's not too busy to put Jehovah first," she said, turning her head and looking out the window.

The rest of the ride was silent.

16

Less than an hour later, we were sitting in the doctor's office waiting for them to come in.

I put a hand on my mother's. "Are you okay?"

It was a dumb question, and I knew that the minute that it left my mouth.

"I'm sorry, of course you're not okay."

My mom just smiled at me. "It's fine hunny, I'm nervous too. But all we can do is pray and lean upon Jehovah."

I turned my head, hoping she wouldn't be able to see my expression. Yeah, pray. Lots of good that has done.

Thankfully the doctor came in. "Mrs. Marquette," he said, taking a seat behind his desk.

"Doctor Householder," she said, gesturing to me, "this is my daughter, Emily."

Householder? My attention snapped to the doctor, and I almost gasped at the similarities between his face and Antony's. It was like I was looking at an Antony from thirty years in the future.

"It's nice to meet you, Emily."

I mumbled something about it being nice to meet him, but I was lost in my thoughts. I knew nothing about Antony's parents. I assumed they were both Witnesses, but now I wasn't so sure.

My thoughts were brought back to the room when my mother gripped my hand. I looked at her, and her face was stoic, but I could see the fear in her eyes. Oh god, what had the doctor said?

"What are my options," my mother's voice cracked as she asked.

The doctor sighed. "I think we should start chemotherapy immediately, and I think that given you are well under sixty there is a good chance that we may have success. I won't sugar coat it, Mrs. Marquette, the survival rate is less than thirty percent in most cases."

I heard my mom's breath shudder, and I felt her squeeze my hand. No. No, no, no. This couldn't be happening.

"But," the doctor continued, "with aggressive treatment you should be able to have at least another five years, if not more. We are constantly making progress with treatments, and the chances of a better outlook even a year from now is likely."

My mother sniffed, and the doctor held out a tissue box for her. She wiped her eyes, then her nose.

"Thank you, doctor."

He cleared his throat. "Now, Mrs. Marquette, I know that you are one of Jehovah's Witnesses, and I am familiar with your stand on blood transfusions. Right now, I think we can do the chemotherapy without you needing any transfusions. However, I do want to warn you that if your red blood cells drop any lower, the only way that we will be able to continue with your treatment will be if you are willing to accept a transfusion. I can assure you that whatever you choose I will respect your choice, and I can also assure you that whatever you choose will be between us. No one," he glanced at me, "other than you and I will know if you decide to take a transfusion."

My mother straightened in her seat. "Absolutely not. Jehovah, my god, would know. I will not take any blood."

The doctor nodded. "Well, as I said, for now it's not an issue; I just wanted to make sure that you were aware that it could likely be an issue in the future."

He was being respectful of my mother's wishes, but I could see the concern in his eyes. My mother very possibly could need blood to save her life, and she was going to allow her belief in a God that had done nothing to save her from this sickness, to stop her from accepting it.

Doctor Householder stood. "I will give the two of you a moment. When you are ready, please see Stacy outside and she will schedule your first treatment. I've already told her that I'd like it to be Wednesday at the latest."

When he left, I turned to my mom. I pulled her into me, and she sobbed. I don't know how long we sat there, the two of us crying, before she sniffed once and pulled back from me. Before it even registered what she was doing, she started praying.

I was so thankful that she had her head bowed and her eyes closed, because she could not see the anger that I knew I couldn't hide.

If she had looked at me in that moment, my fury would have been clear, and she would have been so disappointed. I began crying again, and I forced myself to put on a façade. I knew that this was something I would have to do a lot of in the weeks, months and hopefully years, to come.

I was angry. I was angry at her for being willing to sacrifice herself if it came to that, I was angry at her doctor for ruining our lives, I was angry at my father for not being here, and I was angry at Jehovah for letting my mother get sick.

I drove home without putting any thought into driving. For all I knew, I may have run every red light. When we pulled into the garage and I turned the car off, I looked at my mom. She too looked dazed.

"Mom?"

No response. "Mom," I repeated.

"Yes," she said without turning to me.

"What can I do?"

She smiled, still not looking at me. "You've been doing so much to help me already. I wouldn't have made it through the last year without you and your father. Just keep being there when I need you and keep praying for me."

Guilt trickled into me. I hadn't prayed for anything in months. Well, I suppose that wasn't entirely true; I had prayed after Antony and I...did what we did at the convention, but that was out of fear. It felt empty and hollow, like I was talking to no one.

Maybe if I had prayed more, my mom wouldn't be sick. Maybe if I hadn't done what I did, her sickness wouldn't be cancer.

I could have slapped myself. What the fuck was I talking about? Prayer was doing nothing. Prayer had done nothing to save Brother Stevens last year when he was diagnosed with lung cancer. And he was an Elder.

If Jehovah wouldn't save an elder, then why would he save my mother? No, the only thing that would help her was fighting.

"Of course," I said hesitantly. "But, mom, what if your doctor is right and you end up needing a transfusion?"

My mother turned to me for the first time since we had parked. "Then I will leave that in Jehovah's hands. I really hope that you aren't suggesting that I should take a transfusion?"

"No, mom, I'm just scared."

"Me too," she said with a smile. "All the more reason to throw our burdens on Jehovah."

She unbuckled and opened the car door. "Now, let's get dinner started before your dad gets home."

Dinner was tense. We had broken the news to my dad when he got home, and there were more tears. He had apologized over and over to my mother and I for not being able to go with us to the appointment.

He had owned a small grocery store, but when my mom got sick he had agreed to sell it to a bigger company as long as they let him stay on and manage it. The idea had been that he would have more time to spend with my mom, but it seems like he's gone even more now than he was before.

I knew that it wasn't his fault that he wasn't there, but I was angry anyway.

"Her appointment is at nine on Wednesday. Will you be able to make it?"

My tone must have been harsher than I intended because he looked as if my words cut him.

"Yes, of course. I've already told work that I won't be available for the next couple of weeks."

I just nodded. None of us were really eating, we just kind of moved the food around our plates in silence for what felt like an eternity.

"I'm going to lay down," I finally said, taking my plate into the kitchen.

I went upstairs and texted Antony. He had messaged me around lunch time, but I didn't respond. I hadn't had anything to say really. I still didn't, but I wanted someone to talk to.

Me: Sorry, been busy. How r u

I tossed the phone on my nightstand and lay down on my bed. I felt like I was supposed to be crying, but I just felt numb. Even my earlier anger felt like a distant memory. I felt numb and I hated it.

Antony: It's okay, I understand. I'm alright, long day at work, just getting off and heading home. How is your mom?

It was almost seven o'clock, which meant he had worked a long day again. I'm sure the last thing he wanted to do was hear about the day we had, but I needed to get the weight off of me, even if only a little.

Me: Not good.

Antony: Want to call?

I started to say yes, then I deleted the text and started to call him, then I stopped.

Me: Idk tbh

What did I want? I wanted to talk to him yes, but I also wanted to lay here in silence. What I really wanted was him to be here with me, just holding me and letting me cry, or scream, or fall asleep in his arms.

Antony: I get it. I'm here if you need me.

Irrational anger spiked in me.

Me: You get it? Your mom is dying of cancer and you can't do anything about it?

I regretted sending the text almost immediately; I regretted it even more when I got his response.

Antony: I do get it. My dad got sick when I was 7, and the cancer took him when I was 10.

Fuck. As if I couldn't feel any worse today.

Me: I'm sorry. That was bitchy of me. I didn't know.

Me: It's weird, because I actually thought her doctor might be your dad.

The doctor had looked so much like Antony, I had thought sure he must be his father.

Antony: It's okay. I'm not mad, I just want you to know that I do understand at least some of what you're going through. And not my dad, but that is my uncle. I didn't know what doctor you were seeing or I would've told you.

Me: Oh. Well I'm still sorry. But at least that explains why he looked like you.

Antony: Yeah, I guess lol

The idea of Antony in the shower stirred me. I thought about how incredible he had looked surrounded by steam, hot water running down his naked body.

I had been numb to everything today, everything except anger, and this was neither anger nor numbness. This brought heat between my legs and made my heart race.

I slid my hand down my stomach and between my legs, feeling the anger start to fade even more. I poured myself into my fantasy, and soon the only thoughts I had were of Antony and I naked. I reached over and pulled my dildo from its hiding place under my nightstand drawer.

I don't know how long I had been using it when I heard a gasp from the far end of my room. I pulled the sheets over myself as I locked eyes with my mother.

"What the fuck are you doing," I practically shouted.

The words were out before I could think. The look on my mother's face was one of utter rage, mixed with extreme disappointment. She had never heard me curse, and she had no way of knowing that I had a dildo.

"I'm sorry," I choked out.

Before I knew what was happening my mother was standing over me, slapping me over and over again.

My parents had barely given me spankings when I was a child, and I could not remember the last time that my mother had struck me. The shock of it made me just lay there, naked and wide eyed, as my mother continued to slap me.

"Who are you," she asked through sobs when she finally stopped slapping me.

I pulled the blankets over myself and shrank to the other side of the bed. My skin stung all over, I could taste blood in my mouth, and my heart was breaking for my mother. The same mother that had just beaten me.

"Mom, I'm me, what kind of question is that?"

She shook her head violently. "No, my Emily would never swear, she would never do," she gestured to my dildo now laying at the foot of my bed, "that. My Emily loves Jehovah and serves him faithfully."

Anger at that spiked through me. "I did love Jehovah, and I have served him faithfully. And so have you and dad. And where has that gotten you? You're dying, and one of the only things that might save your life your God won't allow you to use, because he'd rather see you die than use science."

Fear ran through me as anger flashed in her eyes again. "You would blame Jehovah for my illness? Have we not raised you better than that?"

I was about to answer when I heard my father's voice from my doorway. I don't know how long he stood there, or what he had witnessed, but he must have heard my last words.

"Get out of my house," he said, turning and walking away.

"Dad," I called after him, but he ignored me.

"Mom," I said turning to her, "I'm sorry, I shouldn't have said that, I'm angry."

"You're angry," my mother scoffed with the last of her strength, "I'm the one that is dying. And I'm angry too, but I know that the one I need to be angry with is Satan and his wicked world, not

Jehovah. I have stayed strong through all of this knowing that when I am resurrected in paradise, I will see you and your father again. But now…"

"Mom," I said quietly when she trailed off.

"No. Your father is right. Leave."

Her slaps had hurt, but nothing compared to the feeling of being slapped by my parents' words.

"Mom, where am I supposed to go?"

"You're an adult. Figure it out; And leave your keys here. You won't need them."

"I can't take the car? It's almost nine o'clock at night, what am I supposed to do?"

She shrugged as she left my room and started back down the stairs.

"You have ten minutes to pack a bag, and then I want you out of my house," she called from somewhere downstairs.

Fifteen minutes later I was walking down a dimly lit street in our Avon subdivision, a backpack full of clothes and the charger for my phone. Thankfully, my phone was fully charged.

I tried to call Rebecca, but it went to voicemail.

Me: Hey I need u. Please call

I was scared, I felt more alone than I ever had, and I didn't know what to do. I walked to the gas station up the road from our home.

Me to Antony: Call as soon as u can plz

I sat on the curb of the parking lot and sobbed. What was I going to do? Not even just tonight, what about tomorrow? What about for a car? What about for a home? How am I going to get my hours for the ministry?

The ministry? What the hell was I thinking? Fuck the ministry. I'm over it, and I'm not going to worry about any of that right now. By the time I find a way to the next meeting, the elders would have heard about what happened and I was sure that I would be removed from the pioneer list anyway.

My whole world felt like it was crashing down around me. I had never in my life thought of suicide, but in that moment, the thought crossed my mind.

I didn't want to die, but this was all too much. I couldn't breathe all of a sudden. I was vaguely aware that my phone was ringing, but it sounded like it was coming from underwater. I must have hit answer, because I could hear a voice on the other end.

"Hello? Hello? Are you there?"

That perfect voice pulled me out of whatever haze I was in enough to respond.

"I got kicked out, I don't know where..."

That was all I could get out before I began sobbing again.

"Baby, where are you?"

That was only the second time that he had ever called me anything other than my name. How could such a small thing feel so good right now? I actually smiled for a split second.

"I'm at...the gas station...right by 90," I got out between sobs.

"Okay, I'll be there in a half hour. I'm on my way, stay on the phone with me."

"No, no it's fine, just focus on driving, I'm okay, I'll be okay. Just get here," I managed to stop crying long enough to say.

As soon as I hung up the phone, I got a text.

> **Becca: I can't call, what's wrong?**

> **Me: Nothing. Everything. It's fine. Got kicked out.**

It took a minute for her response to come, and I just sat there looking at the road. This was unbelievable. I tried to trace back how I actually got to this point, homeless and sitting on a curb at a gas station.

I couldn't think straight. Nothing made sense. I had never in my life imagined that my parents would kick me out of our home. Their home, I guess, not mine.

> **Becca: OMG where r u**

**Me: Gas station. Antony
on his way.**

My phone rang, caller ID showing it was Rebecca.

"What the hell happened," she asked softly.

"I don't know. I took my mom to the doctor this morning, oh yeah, she's got cancer," as soon as the words were out of my mouth I regretted saying them. Fresh sobs began.

"I'm so sorry, Em. Why did they kick you out?

"She found me using my toy."

"What toy," she asked. Before I could answer, it registered. "Oh. Shit. I'm sorry."

I told her the gist of what had happened, and that Antony was coming to get me.

"Antony? You guys are close like that?"

God. There was so much I hadn't told her, so much I couldn't tell her.

"Yeah, I guess. I mean, we've been talking and since I couldn't get a hold of you he was my next thought. I just need picked up."

Becca sighed. "I'm sorry. I'm all the way out in Seven Hills or I'd come get you."

What the hell was she doing out there. "Seven Hills?"

She must have heard the question in my voice. "Yeah, well, you've got your secrets and I have mine."

She said the words softly, but they still stung. She was right of course, I had hidden me and Antony from her, and she hadn't told me that she apparently had a boyfriend in Seven Hills.

I tried to smile so that my voice would be light. "I guess so. I'll tell you all about it sometime. But for now, I just need to figure out what I am going to do."

"Well, let him get you tonight, but don't tell anyone else where you are. I can probably say you were with me if anyone asks. Tomorrow, we'll sort it out."

This time I didn't have to try to smile, it just came naturally. "Thank you. I love you."

"Bitch, I love you too," she said, and I could hear her smile. "Call me if he doesn't pick you up for some reason, and I'll come get you."

I thanked her and hung up. A few minutes later, Antony's hummer pulled into the parking lot. He got out of the truck, and pulled me into a deep hug. We didn't speak, and he just rubbed my hair as I soaked his shirt in tears.

After a few minutes, he pulled back gently from me.

"Come on," he said, "let's get you back to my place and get you comfortable."

It took about a half-hour to get to Sandusky. We didn't speak on the ride, he just held my hand and made sure that I knew he was there for me. When we got off of the highway, he drove for another fifteen minutes or so.

I don't know what I was expecting when I thought of his house, but this was not it.

We turned off the main road and down a rural dirt road. In the distance I could see lights, but as we got closer, I was both stunned and delighted by what I saw.

His home was not a 'house' at all. Nestled in a large clearing, with woods on the backside, sat a large camping trailer. Under the canopy hung soft yellow string lights, with a couple of Adirondack chairs underneath.

"Wow," I said, speaking for the first time since he picked me up.

"It's not much, but it's mine and there's no rent. It was my uncle's, but he sold it to me with the land a couple of years ago. He had planned on building a house here, but he elected to build a winter home in New Mexico instead."

"It's amazing," I said with genuine wonder. "I can't imagine how peaceful it must be living here."

"It is very peaceful. It actually took some getting used to, but now I love it," he said, turning off the engine. "Come on, I'll show you around."

Whatever I had envisioned his bachelor pad to look like, this was not it. The living room couch was full of pillows that matched the drapes, there were bookshelves on either side of the couch full of books, across from the kitchen sat a small table with a candle in the middle.

The camper smelled faintly woodsy, which I attributed to the candle. The only thing that was anything like what I had expected was a decent size TV with an Xbox set up across from the couch.

"This is nice."

He smiled. "Thank you. It's my place to relax. I work all day, and when I come home it's nice to have a calm place to unwind. Can I get you a drink?"

He walked to the kitchen and opened the refrigerator. "I've got soda, water, beer."

"I'll take a water, please," I said as I sat down on the couch.

He brought me the water and sat next to me. "Em, what happened?"

I sat back and blew out a breath. "I took my mom to the doctor this morning, like you know. When we got home, I was upset. It pisses me off that she isn't willing to do everything she can to fight this cancer shit."

"She's not going to fight it?"

I shrugged. "She is, but the doctor, your uncle I guess, said she might need a blood transfusion. And of course, she won't take one. I knew she wouldn't if it came down to it, but I had hoped maybe the reality of her dying would make her think twice."

Antony put his arm around me, and I laid my head in his lap. "My uncle sees it all the time, Witnesses that aren't willing to budge and will face whatever that means."

"What it means is that she'll die," I said, choking back a sob and continued.

"But that's not the point, I guess. I was angry, I felt like my world was crashing, I was feeling numb to everything, so I went upstairs to my room. The only thing that made me feel anything was thinking about you, about what we've been doing. So, I got out my toy and I used it. I don't know if I didn't close the door, or if I just didn't hear my mom, but she caught me. Words were exchanged and she slapped me; at some point my father walked up and he told me to leave. I tried to beg my mom, but she told me I had ten minutes. And so…"

I had trailed off before I started crying again. Antony just rubbed my hair.

"I'm sorry," he said. "I feel like this is my fault. If we hadn't…you know, then maybe they wouldn't have caught you."

I sat up. Was he crazy?

"What? No! You are the *only* thing that has made me feel alive, made me feel even remotely happy, in a very long time. Since my mom got sick, I feel like I've just been waiting, like my life was paused. I've been doing everything I'm 'supposed' to do, meetings and the field ministry, personal study, all of that, but I'm doing it out of habit. It's just become something rote."

He didn't look convinced. He looked like he still felt guilty, as if this was all his fault somehow.

I put my hand on his cheek and smiled at him. "You have changed my life. I'm not trying to sound weird, or clingy, or anything like that, I don't even mean it that way. Just, I don't know, since we met, since the Viking Lodge, I have felt something again. Like my life isn't just me waiting for my mom to get better or not. I was miserable, I wasn't happy at all. I have been mad at God for a long time, and I know that this, what we're doing isn't right, but I don't care. If he doesn't care enough to protect my mom, why should I care? Hell, if he wants me to be unhappy to prove that I'm his loyal servant, then why should I be that servant?"

Antony put his hand over mine. "I…okay, so…" he stammered and couldn't find his words.

"What? Just say it. I was just scarily honest with you. If I'm being too clingy or weird or whatever, just tell me, I can handle it."

He sighed and took my hand off of his cheek and stood up. He walked to his kitchen, shaking his head.

"No, it's not that. I am doing what I do, living this life, being a Witness, for my mom. She would be devastated if she knew how I really felt. And, part of me want's to do it, because yeah, you know what, what if they're right? What if I do get to see my dad again one day in paradise? But I don't believe that. Deep inside I don't. And," he sighed.

"And what," I asked as I stood and walked to him, taking his hand in mine. "Tell me."

"And honestly, when I met you I thought you were the most beautiful woman I had ever seen. I asked Miguel about you, and he basically told me all about what a good Sister you were, and then told me to stay away from you. He didn't want me to be a bad influence on you, I guess. And maybe he was right. Maybe that's all I've done is corrupt you. But I wanted you. I didn't think it would turn in to this, us doing…everything so fast, or whatever. I thought, maybe we would talk. Maybe we would be able to date, and maybe if I tried, I could be a good Brother for you. Maybe you were my key to living the best life, to finding a person to walk side by side with me while we did all of the things we were supposed to so I could see my dad again."

He looked down as he finished.

"And I didn't do that for you," I said, taking a step back.

His head snapped up, and stepped right back to me, his hands gently on my face.

"No, but I don't think that is what either of us needed. What if this is what we needed? What if we needed someone to experience life with? What if we needed someone to help us heal? What if the Witnesses are wrong, and it's all bullshit? What if now was the time we were meant to come together, to find each other, to help each other get free of all of the things we've been tied down to for our whole lives? What if," he kissed me gently and pulled back, "we are each other's best life?"

I buried my face in his chest. "You feel like you are, you feel like you are my anchor in the crazy, turbulent sea that is my life right now. I don't want to let that go," I said as I wrapped my arms around him and squeezed him tight.

He kissed the top of my head. "Then don't. Hold on to me, and I promise you, I will hold on to you. Whatever happens, whatever we go through, whatever our families, or the congregation, or our friends do, we hold each other and never let go."

20

Less than an hour later, I had showered and changed into the pajama shorts and top that I had thrown in my backpack. Antony had already gone up to the bedroom to throw on fresh linens.

"At some point I'm going to have to go home and get my stuff. I don't know where I'm going to put it, or what the hell I'm going to do with it all," I called up to him.

When he didn't answer, I closed my backpack and made my way up the four stairs to his bedroom. He was snoring softly, and I didn't want to disturb him so I slid cautiously into the bed. I was exhausted and wished that I could fall asleep as easily as he had.

He looked so peaceful, lying on his back. I longed for sleep, but when I closed my eyes all I could see was the look on my parents' faces, their words that were full of disgust and disappointment.

'Who are you' my mother had asked. That was an excellent question.

Who was I? A year ago, I could have answered that question. I knew who I was, I recognized myself. That had changed so slowly that I'm not even sure I noticed it until recently.

I had excused the things that I was doing that I knew were wrong: masturbating, cussing, watching porn. Everyone had vices, and I could easily brush them off as things about myself that I needed to work on.

A year ago, they were sins that I prayed about, that I would stop doing for a while before giving back into them. Now though?

My whole life, I was raised to serve Jehovah. But when I thought about doing that now, it made me angry. How does a God that would let his servants suffer and die when he has the power to save them deserve my devotion? How dare he demand that my mother be willing to sacrifice her life to follow his petty rules? What kind of a 'loving father' does that to his children?

I opened my eyes and turned to face Antony. He pulled the blankets higher up on himself and began snoring gently again. I brushed away a lock of curls from his face and smiled.

How could being with the one person that had made me feel something again, that made me happy, truly happy, be wrong? And why did being happy, why did knowing that I would never be willing to give up my life or the lives of my family for a demanding God, make me feel like shit?

Because what you're doing is wrong, how you're feeling is wrong, I could hear my mothers voice say. *Pray to Jehovah, throw your burdens on him, trust in him, and he will help you through. Beg for his forgiveness and he will strengthen you.*

I believed that once upon a time. Not anymore. Now it didn't feel right. My parents had always told me that they converted to the Jehovah's Witnesses because it felt like 'the truth'.

My whole life I had been taught that it was the truth, the one true religion. And it had felt like that for so long, but not anymore. Now it felt wrong, it felt like a lie. How could I help my parents understand that?

Even as I thought the question, I knew they never would. My mother was ready to die for her faith. My parents had kicked me out of their home because of something that felt so small to me, such a minor sin.

They would never understand the fact that what they taught me, what they spent years indoctrinating into me, didn't feel real anymore. Their idea of 'the best life' felt so very far from the actual thing.

And now that I had just a taste of what my best life could be, being happy, feeling like I had someone beside me that supported me, the real me, I could never throw that away.

No matter how much I prayed, no matter how hard I tried, I knew that I could never devote my life to that religion, or their God, again.

At some point I must have fallen asleep. When I woke up again, Antony was still snoring softly, but now it was close. His arm was wrapped around my stomach, and he was curled into me. I felt…oh my god, is this what they mean when they talk about 'morning wood'?

I instantly felt heat rush through my body when I felt his hardness pressed up against my bottom. Was he sleeping nude?

I slid my hand down my shorts and began touching myself. I had planned on just using my hand, but fuck, he felt so good and so hard against me.

21

I slipped out of his arms and pulled back the covers carefully. Antony stirred but didn't wake up. To my utter delight he was sleeping nude, and he was very much hard.

Taking off my shorts and straddling his calves, I took him in my mouth. He moaned with pleasure, and I looked up to see a now smiling Antony looking at me.

"Holy shit," he said as he laid his head back down on his pillow.

I licked up and down the length of him, stopping and sucking one of his balls into my mouth when I would reach the base. He moaned, and arched his back, but didn't say anything.

After a few minutes of using my mouth, I moved my way up his body, taking him in my hand and as I sliding down his shaft. The feeling of him inside of me made me moan loudly, not a care in the world of being heard out here in the privacy of his home.

I rocked back and forth, grinding him as he grabbed my hips and matched my rhythm. I came twice on him before he rolled me over, his head just inside my lips.

"I don't know if I'll be able to come," he said awkwardly.

"I...oh, I'm sorry, I," I stammered. I didn't know what to say to that. "Did I...do something wrong?"

He smiled and came down to kiss me, his full length sliding inside me with ease as he did. He covered my gasp with his lips.

"No," he said when he finally broke the kiss. "Sometimes when I wake up like this, I don't know, it's just hard to come. I'm not sure what the reason is."

"Oh, well, we don't have to-"

My words were cut off when he pulled back and thrust hard into me again.

"I want to, I am just letting you know, we may be at this for a while before I finish."

I reached up and wrapped my arm around his neck, pulling him to me.

"Then fuck me however you want to make yourself come."

He pulled out of me and smiled before rolling me over onto my stomach. His hands gripped my backside and spread my cheeks. Soon he was inside of me again, his body slamming hard and fast against mine. He pulled my hips up and I propped myself onto my elbows.

Before I registered the pain, I heard the 'slap' of his hand on my ass. I screamed out in a mixture of pain and pleasure, and he slapped again.

The mixture of the pure ecstasy of him inside of me, and the sting of his hand on my ass made me bury my face in the pillow and moan.

He kept going, hard and deep, the slap-slap-slap of his hand matching the pace of his thrusts. After a moment, he stopped spanking me and grabbed a fistful of my hair, pulling my head up and off of the pillow.

Holy shit, I had only seen things like this in the videos I'd watched. I had always been half turned on by the idea of being fucked like this, and half scared. The half scared part of me was gone now.

"Yes, fuck me. Fuck me like the little slut I am," I said.

Jesus Christ, there I was again, not recognizing myself, but loving every second of it. That was when I noticed his reflection in the mirror above his headboard. The carnal look in his eyes, the pure pleasure that he was getting out of fucking pushed me over the edge.

"Why aren't you using your finger too" I asked, locking eyes with him in the mirror.

He smiled a wicked smile and released my hair, putting his thumb in my mouth.

"Suck it," he said.

I obliged and a second later, his thumb, wet with my saliva, was inside of me.

"Do you like the way that feels," he asked, low and husky.

The feeling of both of my spots filled, the way his four fingers felt resting on the small of my back.

"Yes, don't stop. I'm going to come."

He didn't, and I did. I went weak, and he used his free hand to wrap under my waist and hold me up while he continued to drive in and out of me.

When I finished, he rolled me over again, spreading my legs and dropping his mouth to my wet pus-wait, no, he stuck his tongue in and out of my other needy spot.

"Oh god," I moaned as I twined my fingers into his hair and propped my legs on his shoulders.

As he continued to tease me with his tongue, I released my hold on his head and grabbed his hand, pulling it to my mouth. I sucked the length of his middle finger and let his hand go.

His mouth moved to my clit as I felt his finger slowly push against me. I pushed back, and felt it start to go in. One knuckle.

He pulled it out and wet it himself before returning his mouth to its task. Again, I felt the pressure. Two knuckles.

I pushed hard against him and felt his finger go all the way inside of me. A second later I felt his thumb slip into my pussy.

I gripped the sheets and moaned. "Don't stop, please don't stop. Fuck, I'm going to come, yes, yes, right there-"

My words were cut off by the wave of pleasure as I came all over his face. He slowly slipped his finger out of me. I pulled him up to me and kissed him deeply. I was beginning to crave the way I tasted on his lips.

When I broke the kiss, he rolled off of me and onto his side. The look on his face would have made me melt if I had any energy left to do so.

"You didn't even come," I said with a pout.

Antony laughed. "I told you, that's not always easy to do in the mornings like this."

I looked away. I felt guilty that I had come so many times, and he never even finished.

"I'm sorry, I feel selfish."

He climbed back on top of me and looked me in the eyes. "Don't ever feel bad for enjoying yourself. I wanted you to come. I love the way you sound, the look on your face, the way your body feels as you orgasm. Trust me, I enjoyed every second of that. And besides," he said with a shrug, "we can always try again later if you want."

22

And I did want. But it would have to wait, he needed sleep because he had to get up at five in the morning so that he could leave by six.

When we woke back up, I watched as he got dressed, my eyes soaking in his body as he had gotten out of the shower and begun putting on his work clothes. There was something sexy about his stained outfit, like it made him more manly looking than anything else that I had seen him in.

"Do you like my rags," he asked with a smile as he noticed me watching.

"They are the sexiest rags I've ever seen," I said, biting my lip.

"Don't start or you'll make me late," he said with a laugh. "Do you want to drive me to the shop, so you can use my truck for stuff today?"

I shook my head. "No, I don't think I need to go anywhere. I'm going to just call Rebecca and try to explain some of what happened."

"Oh, yeah, about that. You won't get great service out here. You can use my landline if you want," he gestured to a cordless phone behind his TV, "but it will show up on caller ID, so she'll know where you're calling from."

I shrugged. I hadn't told him that she already knew where I was.

"That's fine. How do you have a landline out here?"

"When my uncle was going to build a house, he had electric, water, all the utilities run. So, I just put them in my name."

He sat on the small couch and started to put on his grass-stained boots.

"Are you sure you don't have just a few minutes," I said as I took the boot from his hand and dropped it, straddling him.

"I can't be-"

His words were cut off when I pulled my shirt over my head and raised an eyebrow.

"Yes, I'm pretty sure I have a few minutes," he said before kissing me.

Twenty minutes later, he was driving away, and I was alone in his home. I hadn't bothered to dress after we had sex, and I half expected him to delay leaving again. But he didn't.

I didn't think I would be lonely, but the instant his truck was out of my sight, I felt more alone than I ever had.

Me: Hey, sorry I didn't call. I'll call you in a few minutes, going to take a shower real quick.

While I waited for Becca to text me back, I went into his bathroom and turned on the water.

I walked back into his kitchen to see if he had cereal, or donuts, or anything really. He did have cereal, but it was incredibly boring, no sugar flakes. I'd rather be hungry. I heard my phone buzz.

Becca: Okay. I need some answers. Your mom called my mom this morning freaking the fuck out.

I just tossed my phone down and took my shower. A small part of my felt guilty that my mother was 'freaking the fuck out', but more of me was indifferent. How could she make me leave in the middle of the night like that?

No, let her freak out. Let her feel a little bit of the pain that I felt at being told to leave. This was her choice, hers, and my father's. They are the ones that wanted me out.

I finished my shower and dried off. Grabbing Antony's phone on my up to the bedroom, I laid back on his bed. God it still smelled like him, and a fresh wave of loneliness washed over me. I dialed Rebecca's number.

"Hello," she answered after the second ring.

"Hey, it's me."

"I want details," she said with a fake demanding tone.

"Okay, okay," I laughed. I started to talk, and she cut me off.

"No, better yet, I'm coming to you."

I didn't think Antony would care. "Okay, but bring donuts or something, I'm starving. Do you need directions?"

"No, I've been there with Miguel before, give me an hour," she said before hanging up the phone.

One hour. I had the next hour to myself, with nothing to do. I rolled on to my side and rested my head on Antony's pillow. The scent immediately let me know exactly what I would do to pass the time.

***

Not even an hour later, I heard the gravel of Antony's driveway. I threw on my pajama shorts and top and peaked my head out. Rebecca was just getting out of her car, a box of donuts in her hand.

"Thank god," I said running out and grabbing the donuts.

"Nice to see you too," she said as I skipped back into the camper.

"Ew, it's so…bachelor-ish," she said, waving a hand around the home as she walked in behind me.

"Well, he was a bachelor," I chuckled through a bite of my custard donut.

"Was," she asked, cocking her head.

"Was."

"Are you guys like, official then?"

"Yeah, I guess we are. We talked about it before I got kicked out, but I think now it's definitely going to be out there sooner than later."

"Oh my god," she said, lowering her voice and glancing up to the bedroom, "did you guys have sex?"

My hesitation was answer enough.

"Bitch, what," she squealed. "You better give me details, and start from the beginning."

Rebecca had wanted details, and details I gave her. We sat on Antony's couch, and I had intended to leave out the parts where Antony and I had had sex.

But, in the end, she was my best friend and I found that I couldn't lie to her, even if only by omission.

By the time I was done, and had finished with my parents kicking me out of my home, I was in tears. Rebecca grabbed hold of me and hugged me tight, not saying anything.

After a moment, she pulled back from me and looked me in the eye.

"Do you love him?"

I opened my mouth to answer, but immediately closed it again. I should say yes, right? I should say that I very much loved him, that he had been a light in the dark storm that had been my life recently.

But she wasn't just asking if I loved him. She was asking if I was in love with him. And that I didn't know.

"I don't know. He's amazing, he's gorgeous, the sex is fucking mind blowing although it's not like I have anything to compare it to, and he has been there for me every time I've needed him. But," I paused and looked down, "I've only known him for less than a week. Which is fucking crazy, and I'm scared that this will all wear off."

"Good," Rebecca smiled. "If you had said yes, I would have smacked you and dragged you out of here right now and taken you... I don't know where, but we'd have left."

I looked at her with confusion. "What do you mean? Shouldn't I love him?"

She scoffed. "Why? Because he's cute, and he's been super sweet to you, and you're sleeping with him? No."

"I," I closed my mouth because I wasn't sure what to say. "Well," I tried again and stopped.

"Em," she said, putting her hands on my shoulders. "You've known him since Saturday. It's Tuesday. He is the first man to get his dick wet in you. My god, if you told me you loved him, I would tell you that you were insane. But," she smiled, "none of that means that you won't love him. You two may spend the rest of your lives together, or the universe may have sent him to you because he is what you need now and when the time comes you will both move on."

"The universe," I asked, raising an eyebrow.

Rebecca sighed and let go of my shoulders. "Em, I haven't been there for you like I should have recently. I've got a lot going on, and I haven't seen the woman you are now, the way you've changed. If I had, I'd have talked to you about this a lot sooner."

I slid back a little bit on the couch to be able to look at her more directly. "Talked to me about what?"

"You aren't the only one that has had doubts. I haven't believed in any of this in a very long time."

"What," I asked incredulously. "What do you mean 'doubts', and how long?"

"A couple of years, maybe a little more."

"And you never told me," I was shocked and hurt that she would keep this from me.

She stood, my look must have been clearly conveying my feelings.

"How could I? What would I say? 'Hey, Em, I don't think that this is the truth, I don't even think I believe in God'?"

"You're my best friend," I said, my voice raising just a little. "So, yeah, honesty would be nice."

Rebecca caught my tone and volume, and matched it. "Honesty? Like you gave me this weekend? If your parents hadn't kicked you out, would you have even told me any of what you've been doing?"

I looked down, knowing she was right. I would've hid everything from her.

"Exactly," she said. "And why?"

"I…I didn't want to get in trouble. And I didn't want to lose you," I answered, my eyes dampening just a little.

"Not just me. You didn't want to lose every fucking person that you have loved for your whole life," she said, her tone softening. "And who would?"

She sighed and sat back down beside me, taking both of my hands in hers.

"But I should've been there for you. I should've made sure that you knew, no matter what, I love you and I will always be your best friend. But this goddamn cult, this is what it does. I've been talking to a bunch of people on the internet lately, and there are so many of us out there. We call ourselves 'PIMO's',

Physically In Mentally Out. Everyone has different reasons for staying a part of the organization, but most of us do it for family, for friends. No one wants to lose their parents, grandparents, children, aunts and uncles, everyone they know, just because they don't agree with the teachings of a bunch of men in Brooklyn anymore."

I was at a loss. I thought I was the only one, the only one that felt like this was all bullshit, the only one that would have stayed just for the sake of holding on to the people I loved. How egotistical of me. Of course, I wasn't the only one.

"Em, I will never abandon you because we don't believe in the same things. I have found so many friends, real true friends that will be there no matter what I believe. You are my first friend, and the truest of all. Hell, you're the first girl I had a crush on and probably the first one I fell in love with."

My head snapped up, and my jaw dropped. "What?!"

Rebecca smiled at me. "You heard me, bitch," she said, gently touching my cheek. "I fell in love with you. And then, when you asked me about boys, and toys, and all of the things that you were feeling, I knew that you would never love me like that. So I pushed my feelings away, buried them down. You are my best friend in the entire universe. We weren't meant to be more. And I am fine with that. I love you, and always will, as if you were my sister. Not the bullshit 'Sister' that people at the hall call each other, but truly my sister. I would do anything for you, and I would defend you to anyone."

My eyes burned again with tears at her words, but my mind was still processing what she had just said to me.

"You…you're like…"

"Gay? Yes," she chuckled, "I am a lesbian. And when I realized that, it started me on a path that lead to me waking up and realizing that maybe the Jehovah's Witnesses didn't have 'the truth'."

"But, you always were flirting with boys. Everyone said you were boy crazy, you knew that, the Elders even talked to you about it."

She smiled, but it was a sad smile. "Yeah. Well, when you hate yourself because you feel like you are an abomination to God, you do everything you can to try to change. I tried to like boys. I messed around with them, I did things I'm not proud of, not because of God but because it wasn't who I really was. I tried to pray, I begged Jehovah not to do this to me, not to make me something that he hates. Do you know how it feels to believe you're going to die just because of who you love?"

I pulled her into a hug. "No, I don't. But you are perfect," I said, squeezing her tight.

"Oh, I know that now," she said with a genuine smile. "But it took me years and lots of true friends, to help me understand that."

I was still in shock. "So all of the boys?"

"Just a cover, just me trying to be what I thought I was supposed to be."

"And you never told anyone?"

Her smile faded. "I did. I told my parents, and they made me talk to the Elders. The Elders were…harsh. I said the things they wanted me to say, I acted the way they wanted me to act, and they decided I had repented of my 'disgusting ways'. One of them even…"

Her voice trailed off. "Even what, Becca?"

"One of the Elders met with me alone. He had told my mom that he wanted me to come over to his house for a shepherding call. I thought it was going to be more of the same. But he told me that I just hadn't found the right man, because I was only talking to boys. I was sixteen, Em. Sixteen, and he was in his forties. I thought maybe he was right, and then when he kissed me, I didn't fight him off. I even remember praying as it was happening that Jehovah would let me feel aroused by him. How fucked up is that?"

"Bec-", I started, but she held up a hand.

"No, listen, or I won't be able to get it out. I need to say it to someone. He kissed me, then he asked me if that 'made me wet'. When I just shook my head, he smiled and said that it was okay. I just needed more. He unzipped his pants. That was the first time I had seen a penis in real life, and I was no more interested in it then than I was when I saw it on the internet. But…but he told me that it would help me if I sucked him. And I don't know what I was thinking, I shouldn't have, but there was that small part of me that wanted to not be gay. So I did. I sucked him for what felt like forever, before he asked me again if I liked it, if I was getting wet."

Becca paused and looked at the floor. "When I said no, he said that it was okay, and he got up and left the room. I thought that was it, I was done, he knew that I wouldn't ever be interested in boys that way. But he came back a second later and he had something in his hand. It was lube, Em. He said that I just needed something to help 'get me started'."

Becca sobbed and I pulled her in for a hug.

"It's okay, you don't have to tell me, you don't have to think about it, to relive it again."

She pushed me back. "I don't have to think about it? There isn't a fucking day that has gone by that I haven't thought about it. I have to see that fucking animal at every goddamned meeting. I have to sit there, while he gives talks and prays and does all of the things that he does in that fucking church knowing what he did to me. No," she said, straightening, "no, I need to tell you, I need you to know."

She wiped her eyes, and continued, her voice hard and determined now.

"He took me to his bedroom, and told me to take my clothes off. I wish every single day that I had left when he first kissed me, but I didn't. I did what he said. Maybe if I did what he told me, I'd like boys or maybe he'd tell my parents that I was better, that I was forgiven. He took his clothes off, and put the lube on his fingers, rubbing it on his disgusting dick. He pushed me down onto the bed and then he shoved his fingers in me, pouring more of the lube, before he…he got on top of me and forced his disgusting fucking dick in me in one thrust. It hurt so bad, and I hated every second of it. I think that was when I started crying, and I don't really remember how long he did that to me for. But when he was done, he told me to pray that Jehovah forgive me for having lustful thoughts about other girls, and that I should pray for him to make me love men like I was designed to."

"Jesus Christ," I said, wiping her tears away. "Did you tell anyone?"

Becca laughed humorlessly. "I told my mom. She said that I was just trying to take attention off of my sins and make an elder look bad. My own mother didn't fucking believe me."

"I'm so sorry, Becc," I said, but it felt so very hollow even in my own ears.

There was nothing that I could say that could even come close to comforting her.

"It's okay," she said, wiping her eyes and trying to smile. "I told him at the next meeting that if he ever tried to touch me again, I would tell the police. He has barely spoken to me since."

"Who did this to you?"

Becca shook her head furiously. "No, I don't want to face him again, I don't want to dig it back up with other people again. I don't want anyone else to know. I don't want to ever have to talk about it with anyone that I don't choose to tell. It's better this way."

I pulled her in and held her, letting her sob into me.

I just sat there holding Rebecca for what felt like an eternity before she stopped crying and pulled her face back, her eyes puffy and red, her cheeks stained with tears.

"Let me get you some tissue," I said, standing and going to the kitchen.

"I'm sorry, I didn't mean to bring more drama and negativity to you right now. I just, I don't know, I felt like I needed to tell you everything, why I feel the way I do about that fucking cult, since you had been so open and honest with me," she said as she took the tissue from me.

"I'm glad you told me," I said, sitting back down next to her. "I'm so sorry that you had to go through that."

"But I didn't *have* to go through that, that's the point. I went through that because I was taught to be ashamed of who I was. I was taught that I was something wrong, and horrible, and worthy of only destruction by God. I went through that, I was raped, because of the bigotry of the cult and the man that raped me got away with it because I wasn't believed, because they would rather cover up my rape then 'bring reproach on Jehovah's name'. I hate what he did to me, but it showed me how wrong this religion, this cult, that we have been indoctrinated into by our parents, really is. I may have never woken up if not for what happened. He took something from me, something I can never get back, but I used that pain to harden myself and make sure no one ever does that to me again."

I looked at her. I had never been more proud to have her as my best friend. She was the strongest person I knew. If that was me, I would have crumbled.

Rebecca had hated herself; she was raped by a man that was supposed to help her heal her relationship with God, and she somehow had put on a brave face and never shown an ounce of the pain that she was suffering.

"What?"

I must have been staring for a little too long. "Nothing, I was just thinking how strong you are."

Rebecca shook her head and looked down. "No, if I was strong, I would have told you before. I would have told everyone what he did to me. I'm a coward, and I hate myself for that almost as much as I hated myself for liking women."

I took her hand. "Becca, you are not a coward. There is no right or wrong answer when someone betrays you the way that he did. And you did tell your mother, you did try to expose him for who he is, but she didn't believe you."

That made me angry. Fuck, I was so tired of being angry.

"You know I love your mom, but what the hell kind of a mother doesn't believe her own daughter."

She raised her eyes back to me. "The same kind that would sacrifice herself for a bullshit no-blood rule or beat her daughter because she is exploring her sexuality. A mother that has been brainwashed for years by a cult."

I just shrugged. "We need a distraction. Let's go thrifting. I need some clothes for a couple of days until I can get my stuff from home," I paused and then corrected, "from my parent's home. So, let's have some retail therapy."

Becca's eyes lit up. "Yes! I love retail therapy!"

***

An hour later, I was dressed and we were stopping at our first thrift shop of the day. We went in and walked around, trying on outfits, and thinking about nothing except the moment we were having. It felt good to just spend time hanging out.

"Oh my god, you need to try this on," Becca said, handing me an outfit.

"It's barely big enough for a toddler," I said exaggeratingly.

She rolled her eyes. "Bitch, you can dress however you want now," she said with a wink. "Show those curves off."

I sighed and went into the dressing room. I pulled on the denim shorts that she had handed me, the pockets hanging down further than the actual fabric of the shorts. I took my top off, and put on the halter top, tying it off.

I looked in the mirror. My first thought was that if anyone from the Kingdom Hall saw me, they would be shocked and run to the Elders. My second thought was: who the fuck cares?

The top was backless and showed off much of my stomach. I wasn't out of shape, but I didn't have perfect abs either. I wasn't sure.

But when I turned and looked at my ass in the mirror, I smiled. The shorts came down to just above the very bottom of my ass cheeks. Antony would absolutely love this outfit.

"Well, come on, let's see it," Becca called from somewhere outside the changing room.

"Okay, okay," I said, walking out tentatively.

"Damn! You are definitely getting that," she said, spinning her finger in a circle for me to show her the back. "Oh, oh yes. That ass has never looked so good!"

"You don't think it's too much? Or, too little I suppose."

Becca gave a mocking gasp and put her hand to her chest. "Oh no, Emily is showing some skin, whatever shall we do?"

I just smiled. "Okay, let me change back."

"Uh-uh, no. Excuse me," she said, turning to one of the workers.

The girl didn't even look up from her phone as she gave a grunt of acknowledgment.

"Can I just pull the tags off of this and she wears it out of the store?"

"I don't care," the girl said, her fingers never stopping from the incessant texting that she was involved in.

"Thank you," Becca said, pulling off the tags. "Go get your stuff, we're going to the mall or something to show you off."

I giggled and went back into the changing room to grab my purse and the clothes I had worn into the store. I stopped when I saw my reflection, my mother's words echoing in my mind.

Who are you?

I smiled at the woman looking back at me.

"I'm a confident, sexy, bad ass bitch," I said out loud as I turned to look at my ass again. I scooped up my belongings and stepped out.

"Yeah you are," Becca said, smacking me on the ass as I walked past her.

"Bitch!"

"Your favorite bitch," she said with a smile, linking her arm in mine. "Where to now? The mall okay, or did you want to go somewhere else?"

"I don't know. I don't have a bunch of money in the bank, and god knows I should save what I do have for a car, but I kind of want to get some makeup."

Becca's eyes lit up. "Oh my god, yes, please? Let me help you!"

I just smiled as we got into the car and headed to the mall.

The whole ten-minute ride to the mall Rebecca went on and on about this makeup style and that. We got out and she linked her arm with mine again.

"There's a new store, it just opened a couple of months ago. We are giving you a makeover!"

She pulled me along excitedly, and we went into the store. I don't know what I was expecting, but this wasn't it. I hadn't been to the mall in at least a year, and when I did go it was just to one of the big box retailers. This was a cute boutique makeup shop with a couple of booths for artists.

"Wait, I thought we were just picking out stuff?"

"Nope," she said with a huge smile.

"Welcome to Delilah's, my name is Amy, what brings you in," the woman at the entrance said when we walked in.

"Hi! My friend is ready to get out of her Jesus faze and I'm getting her a makeover. Make her stunning," she said, pushing me forward. "I'll be back in a few minutes."

When I hesitated, she added, "My treat!"

Well, okay, let's do this, I guess. Amy asked me what style I liked, and I was embarrassed to say that I had never actually worn makeup.

"Oh my! Seriously? Well, we're going to change that! Have a seat."

She showed me pictures of current styles, and I pointed to one of Christina Aguilera.

"Oh, great choice! Let's make you fabulous!"

A half hour later, I was blown away by my own face. I didn't look like a girl that was ashamed of her body anymore. I looked like a woman that knew what she wanted and took it.

"Wow," was all I could manage.

Amy smiled. "Yeah?"

"Yeah!"

"Oh my god," Becca squealed. I hadn't even realized she had come back.

"Yeah," I asked, repeating Amy's question.

"Yeah," Becca exclaimed, repeating my answer.

Becca thanked the woman and we paid and left, a pretty bag full of makeup in hand.

"One more stop," she said, a mischievous smile on her face.

"Oh my god, what more can I do?"

"Come on," she said, linking my arm again. "We're going for a drive."

"Where to," I asked, hesitantly.

"You'll see! Text Antony and tell him he might get home before you, but not to worry, you're with me and we'll be back by eight."

I looked at my phone. It was only just after twelve.

"Okay," I said with a shrug.

Me: Becca came to get me. Going to go do some girl stuff, be back by 8 cant wait to see you :*

A moment later he texted back. I loved how he was always so quick to respond.

Antony: Have fun! I can't wait to see you :*

Oh, if only he knew.

***

An hour or so (and lots of loud singing) later, we were getting off of the highway.

"Seven Hills? It's funny, I thought maybe you were seeing a boy here when you said you were here last night," I said, looking around at the fancy buildings.

Becca smiled a huge smile. "Not a boy."

"Oh my god, you have a girlfriend? For how long? Where? Here?"

"Yeah, her dad owns a few of the dealerships around Cleveland, and I met her when I got my car," she said, her smile never fading.

"That was almost a year ago!"

"I know. I wanted to tell you, I just didn't know how."

In truth, a year ago I may have not taken that well. I may have told the Elders, even shunned her if she got disfellowshipped. God, what the fuck was wrong with me to do that to my best friend?

As if reading my expression, she put her hand on mine. "It's fine, I get it. I'm just glad we're here now. I want the two top girls in my life to meet. And she's a hair stylist, so your makeover will be complete."

I almost teared up. The shame sat heavy in my heart at knowing that my best friend wanted so badly for me to know the woman she loved, but couldn't tell me about because I would've ruined her life.

"I'm sorry," I said.

"No, cut that shit out. It is what it is. We're going forward, you and me, and Antony, and Louisa."

"Louisa," I said, raising an eyebrow. "That's a pretty name."

"And she's a pretty woman," Becca said with a giggle.

We arrived at 'La'count Salon', and walked in.

"Babe," an absolutely beautiful woman exclaimed as soon as we walked in.

Becca kissed her quickly and turned to me. "Babe, this is Emily, Em, this is Louisa."

Louisa was tall, her perfect figure hugged at every curve by a black dress. She had long, rainbow colored hair and dark, smokey makeup.

"It's nice to meet you," I said, extending my hand.

She pulled me into a hug. "You too! Beccs has told me so much about you!"

"Really," I asked, somewhat surprised.

"Oh my god, yes. You mean the world to her, and she talks about you all the time."

I smiled and looked at Becca. I don't think I had ever seen her so happy. Her smile was bigger than I had ever seen, her energy lighting up the room.

"So, Beccs says you're getting your hair done," Louisa said, walking around me and looking at my hair. "What are we doing to it?"

I shrugged. "I don't know. I like it long, but maybe we can add some color or something."

Louisa smiled. "Of course. I think blonde highlights would look incredible, and we could curl it, make it bounce."

I didn't hate the idea. But.

"Can you do it like yours," I asked, somewhat sheepishly.

Her eyes perked up. "Rainbow? Fuck yes we can! Let's go, sit down."

Two hours later, I looked in the mirror and was completely in love with what I saw. I wasn't hiding my body, my hair looked amazing, and I felt like the sexiest woman in the world.

"Oh my god, it looks amazing, thank you," I said, giving Louisa a hug.

"Anything for my girl's girl," she said, squeezing me back.

"Antony is not even going to know what to do with you," Becca said with a huge smile.

"Oh, I think he will know exactly what to do with me."

On the way back to Antony's home, Rebecca received a text from her brother.

Miguel to Rebecca: Hey, gonna stop at Antony's for a beer, he said you and Em might come by?

When Becca told me what he said, I was suddenly self-conscious about my new look.

"I don't know if I want to see Miguel. Did you tell him anything?"

Becca shook her head without looking at me. "No, but I'm sure mom told him about whatever your mom told her."

I shuddered at the thought. "Great. I hope Antony didn't tell him everything."

"Why not? That's his best friend. And you told me everything."

"True," I acknowledged, "but Miguel isn't in the same place we are, is he? I mean, he still believes and wants to follow the Witnesses."

Becca shrugged. "I think so, but that doesn't mean he would stop talking to his friend or turn you guys into the

Elders or anything. I don't know honestly."

"Have you told him about you and Louisa?"

When she didn't respond, I knew that she hadn't. "Exactly."

The rest of the drive was silent. I was lost in thought about all of the possible outcomes of Miguel seeing me like this, or even worse, if Antony had told him we had been sleeping together.

When we got back to to the camper, it was clear I was right to be concerned. As we pulled up we could see Miguel and Antony clearly arguing, their loud voices audible though not discernible, over the sound of the gravel drive.

"Shit," was all Becca said as we parked.

We got out of the car and approached, but neither of them stopped arguing.

"And you would just throw your life away for what, a few minutes of temporary pleasures of the flesh," Miguel roared at Antony.

I could feel my face heat at his words. "Hey," I shouted, "what is going on?"

Miguel spun to face me, as if only now realizing that we had arrived.

"How could you? Who are you? Why," he asked quickly, a look of disgust on his face.

When my mother had asked similar questions, I was hurt. This time, I wasn't hurt; I was angry.

"I'm the same person that I was a month ago," I snapped. "Or six months ago, or a year ago."

Miguel looked at me. "No," he shook his head, "that Emily would never wear those clothes. She wouldn't be sleeping with some guy she just met. She would be at home, caring for her mom and probably preparing for the next day's preaching."

I scoffed. "That Emily has been long gone. I'm not going to pretend anymore to be someone I'm not. I'm still the same person I was, but unlike you, I'm not defined by a fucking religion anymore. I'm not letting an organization that would see my mother die before taking life-saving measures, tell me how I should dress, or who I should sleep with."

Miguel shook his head. "Then you aren't Emily at all," he said, turning to Antony. "You know, I warned her not to talk to you because you were trouble, I was worried that you would make her do something she would regret. But I guess maybe she was just a slut all along."

Before I could respond, Antony's fist connected with Miguel's face. In an instant, they were on the ground, rolling around and trading blows.

"Enough," Rebecca yelled at them, grabbing Miguel and pulling him away from Antony.

"That is your best friend," she said, gesturing to Antony as he stood and brushed himself off. "Are you really going to throw that away? And watch how you talk about *my* best friend."

"Becca," he said, calming just a little. "They are turning their backs on Jehovah. What they are doing is wrong. They are going to die if they don't stop this insanity."

I was about to yell at him, to tell him that Jehovah turned his back on my mom first, but Rebecca spoke before I could.

"What they are doing is fucking normal. What they are doing is living life. You think that they are 'wrong' because they had sex? Guess what Miguel," she said, stepping right into his face. "I have too, but I'm sleeping with a woman, and she's amazing, and she makes me happy, and I've never once felt the way I do when I'm around her."

The look of shock on Miguel's face was almost sad. He staggered back, shaking his head over and over.

"You all are supposed to be my family, my closest friends. I don't know any of you."

He turned and began walking to his car.

"Miguel," Becca called after him. "Miguel, we are your family and your closest friends. Why can't you understand that and love us for who we are?"

Miguel didn't turn as he got in his car. "No, I don't know any of you. You're all dead to me."

The three of us stood silently watching his car speed off down the gravel driveway. When he disappeared from sight, Rebecca began sobbing.

Antony went over and put his arm around her. "Come on, let's get you inside," he said, guiding her into the camper.

He sat her on the couch and went to get tissues from the kitchen.

"Becca, I'm sorry," I said, holding her in a hug.

She didn't pull away, her voice muffled by my top.

"It's not your fault. I guess we're both homeless now."

I hadn't even thought about the repercussions she would face over what just happened. Her mother would undoubtedly do the same thing that my parents had done, kicking her out and having harsh words to say when she did.

Antony came down and hugged us both. "Look, we'll figure this out. I'm sorry that I said anything to him, I just…I just lost my cool when he started yelling at me about letting Em stay here and I tried to explain things, hoping he would understand. I'm sorry."

Antony stood and left, leaving me and Becca crying in each other's arms.

27

It wasn't even ten minutes before Rebecca's phone rang. She looked at the caller ID and tossed the phone onto the TV stand.

"You want me to answer it," I asked, glancing to see that it was her mother that was calling.

Becca just shrugged.

"Hello," I answered softly.

"I raised you better than this," her mother immediately started, her voice a shout through the static of the connection.

"This isn't Rebecca," I said, interrupting her.

There was a pause. "Emily? Ha, of course it is. Tell me, did you corrupt my daughter, or did the two whores just gravitate to each other?"

I stood and left the camper, Rebecca staying where she was on the couch.

"How dare you," I snapped. "Your daughter is not a whore, and neither am I."

"No? Then how do you explain what your mother saw? How do you explain what Miguel just told me happened at that boy's house? You're having sex with him, and my daughter is having sex with a woman. You are both vile in the eyes of Jehovah, no better than two little Jezebels."

"I don't have to explain anything to you, your judgments are meaningless to me. But how can you turn your back on your daughter just because you don't like the person she loves? Your daughter needs you; what kind of a mother are you?"

"You're right," she said, calming. I almost thought that she was going to be reasonable. I was wrong.

"I won't judge you. Jehovah and the Elders will do that. But you are both sinners and unless you change your ways, you will die in Armageddon just like the rest of this wicked world."

"The Elders will judge me? I can live with that. What about how the Elder judged your daughter when he fucking raped her?"

"Lies, just like the lives you've both been pretending to live. No servant of Jehovah, let alone an Elder, would ever do such a thing. You both disgust me."

"Well, that's okay because you disgust me. No real mother would trust a man above her daughter."

"You're both apostates, and I will not listen to this garbage any longer. Let Rebecca know that I will have all of her belongings on the curb by noon tomorrow, and anything that she doesn't come get will be taken by the garbage man."

The call ended before I could say anything. I screamed out, no words, just a scream. Some of the rage and hurt that I had been feeling finally being released.

"What did she say," I heard Rebecca ask quietly from behind me.

I turned to her. "I'm sorry, I didn't realize you were right there."

I went on to tell her what her mother had told me.

Rebecca started crying again, and I pulled her into a hug.

Antony must've heard what I said, because he came from around the side of the camper.

"We can go get your stuff tonight. It's your property, and it is illegal for her to throw it away like that. We can get it tonight, load up my truck and your car, and tomorrow we can figure out what to do with all of it. You can crash here tonight."

Becca smiled and laughed through her tears. "I don't even like you," she said gently.

Antony smiled back. "I know, but you're Em's best friend, so by default you are my friend. Besides," he said, his smile fading "if I hadn't told Miguel about me and Emily this wouldn't have happened."

Becca shook her head. "No, this isn't on you. I knew that this day would come, I have been talking about it with Louisa. I love her, and she loves me, and we were so over hiding that from people. It had to happen anyway."

"Do you want me to call and let your mother know that we are coming," he asked.

She nodded, and I handed him her phone. While Antony called her mother back, I held her.

"We'll be okay," I said, rubbing her hair.

I'm not sure if I was trying to convince her or myself, but either way I knew deep down that it was true. It was going to be impossibly hard, but I knew that we would get through it, and when we had, we would be stronger and happier for it.

A moment later Antony came back. "She said she is leaving, and you have three hours before she comes back. If you're there when she gets there, she will call the police."

"What the fuck," Becca just sobbed into me.

"Come on, let's go," I said, not letting her go.

***

Antony drove his truck, and I drove Rebecca's car. We didn't speak, just drove in silence with an occasional sob from one of us.

True to her mother's word, the house was empty. We helped Rebecca pack everything into our vehicles. The only thing left in her room when we were done was her furniture, which she said she didn't need, and all of her books from the Kingdom Hall.

We were about to lock the front door of the house when she stopped.

"Wait," she said, and ran back in.

I followed her and she began grabbing all of her books and magazines.

"You want these," I asked, Antony and I helping her grab them.

She shook her head. "Follow me."

She led us back through the house, but instead of going to the front, she went into the backyard. She threw her armful of publications into her fire pit. Antony and I followed suit.

"How much time until my mother comes home?"

Antony looked at his watch. "About a half hour."

Rebecca nodded and grabbed the lighter fluid from the house. A few moments later, her fire pit was bright with the burning of leather-bound books, paper magazines and tracts.

Twenty minutes later, the back door of the house opened.

"I warned you, I will call the police," she said from the doorway, before glancing to the fire pit. "What are you doing?

"Come see," Rebecca said calmly.

Her mother came and looked into the fire. Much of the publications had been destroyed, but the covers of some were still clear enough to be made out. She turned to Rebecca and slapped her.

"Get out," she snarled.

The three of us turned and began walking away.

"Burned and destroyed, the same way that your fucking cult destroyed our relationship," Rebecca said without looking back.

28

That night, none of us slept. Rebecca called Louisa and talked to her for hours. I climbed into bed with Antony and we tried to sleep, but emotions were high and sleep was clearly not going to happen.

"Everything is so fucked up," I said, rolling into him and laying my head on his chest.

"Yeah, it's a bit of a mess right now. But it won't be forever. We'll get through this."

I laid there in just my underwear against his shirtless chest and couldn't help but laugh.

"What," he asked, tipping my chin up to look at him.

"I was just thinking, how crazy is this? I'm laying here, in your bed mostly naked, completely comfortable, and we literally met less than a week ago. Everything is moving so fast."

"I'm sorry," he said, clearly misunderstanding me. "I can stay somewhere else while you get on your feet, that way you can have this place and some space."

I rolled on top of him, straddling him and taking his face in my hands.

"I don't want space. I don't think this is a bad thing. I'm just worried that it's moving so fast, and sooner than later it's going to catch up. What if you get sick of me? What if we aren't compatible with each other, and this doesn't last?"

He took my hands. "I'm not worried about me getting sick of you, I'm worried that you'll get sick of me. I love being around you, I love having you here. Yeah, it's going to be an adjustment, and I'm sure we'll have our share of arguments and shit, but I really like you Em. Like, really, really like you. I meant it when I told you that this wasn't just a fling for me, you weren't just 'another girl' to me. You're special, and I want to see what we can be."

I leaned down and kissed him, our bare chests meeting. He pulled me in and kissed me deeply.

"Are you tired," he asked after a moment.

I smiled. "I'm exhausted, but I can't imagine getting much sleep," I said, running my hands down his chest, over his stomach, stopping at the edge of his boxer briefs.

He spun me onto my back and kissed me, moving slowly down my body, kissing my breasts, my stomach,

and running his tongue along the edge
of my underwear.

"We have to be quiet," I said,
lacing my hands in his hair.

"I can be quiet if you can," he
said as he pulled my underwear off.

His gaze stopped on my already
wet slit, and he smiled.

"Fuck you're so perfect," he said,
before his tongue went on to other
things.

We spent the next hour not
thinking about our problems, not
thinking about the religion that was
going to cost us everything and
everyone that we knew now that we
were leaving it. We were in our own
world.

When I finally pulled on my
pajamas and went down to use the
restroom, Rebecca was coming into the
camper.

"The rocking stopped, so I
assumed it was safe," she said with a
knowing smile.

"Oh my god, I'm sorry, I didn't
realize we were rocking it."

"It's fine, get you some," she said,
still smiling.

After I used the bathroom, I came
out and sat next to Becca.

"How are you holding up," I asked, resting my head on her shoulder.

"Honestly? I feel great right now. I'm more worried about how I'm going to feel when it all starts to sink in. When I want to go home, but I can't because it's not my home anymore. Or when I want to call mom or Miguel but can't because they hate me."

"They don't hate you. They are just brainwashed by their beliefs. Maybe they'll come around with time."

She just shrugged. Antony came down and sat at the kitchen table.

"You guys want to watch a movie or something," he asked, gesturing to the TV.

"Sure, what do you have," Becca said, sitting up a little straighter.

I don't remember falling asleep but I woke up still on the couch, a blanket draped over Rebecca and myself. I could hear Antony snoring softly in the bedroom.

Rebecca's head was on my shoulder, and her arm lay across my lap. I felt terrible for her, knowing all too well what she was going through. The only difference was, when I went out in public with Antony, we wouldn't get any looks of disgust for just existing. Not that

I planned on marrying Antony, but I knew that we at least could be married. There was no such option for Rebecca and Louisa.

I tried to slide out of the blanket without waking Rebecca, but she stirred and opened her eyes.

"Hey," she said sleepily.

"Hey."

"What time is it?"

I glanced at the clock on the microwave in the kitchen. "Just after three."

Rebecca rubbed her eyes. "Okay, I'm going back to sleep."

I used the bathroom, and when I came out, Rebecca had curled up on the couch, the blanket pulled to her chin. I slipped past her and climbed into bed with Antony.

When I pulled the covers around me, he turned to me and wrapped me in his arms. I fell asleep knowing that we would all be okay.

***

The next morning, I woke up to the smell of coffee. I rolled out of bed and went into the kitchen, pouring myself a cup. Antony's truck was gone,

and I heard the shower running. I
needed to pee, but I didn't want to go in
while Rebecca was taking a shower.

I stopped at that thought. Why? I
had peed in front of her plenty of times,
we had seen each other naked, and I
had never thought twice about it. Why
did I want to behave differently now?
Just because I knew that she liked girls?

I put my mug down and went into
the bathroom.

"Em? Please tell me that's you
and not Antony," Rebecca called from
the shower.

I just laughed and went about my
business. I grabbed my brush and
started brushing my hair. I could see
Rebecca's shape through the steamed
glass of the shower door.

I wondered for a moment what I
would have done when we were
younger if she had told me that she liked
me. Would I have even considered the
idea? I had come to videos of girls with
girls, but I had never thought about
actually being with a woman. But she
was my best friend and I loved her.

Sadly, part of me knew that what I
would have done was run to the Elders
and told them.

She turned off the water and cracked the door to the shower. "I forgot to grab a towel," she said.

I grabbed her one from the shelf and handed it to her, expecting her to take it and dry off in the shower. She instead stepped out and began drying off, to her nothing was different than any other time we had had a sleepover.

"What," she asked.

I hadn't realized I was staring. "Nothing."

She wrapped the towel around herself, suddenly seeming to be self-conscious.

"Becca," I said, regret in my voice.

"No, it's fine," she said and pushed past me into the camper.

I followed her. "It's not fine, I'm sorry."

She spun on me. "I don't want your apologies. I want you to act like you have a thousand times, like this is no different than any other time we've been around each other. Jesus Christ, we have showered together at the pool how many times?"

She was right. We had gone to the community pool and showered in the locker room dozens of times over the years.

"I'm sorry," I said again.

She tried to go past me to get back into the bathroom to dress.

"I should've never told you," she said, nearly in tears.

I grabbed her hand. "Of course, you should have told me. I just have to get used to it."

"Get used to what? That I like girls, or that I wanted my first time to be with you?"

I dropped her hand and felt my face heat.

"Exactly. I guess it'll never be the same again. But, Em, I'm over you. I knew that it could never work between us because I knew you didn't like girls. And that's fine, but I guess you need time to accept that, and I'll give it to you. Just don't fucking look at me like you're disgusted by me, please."

"Disgusted by you," I repeated, shocked. "I'm not at all, and never have been. I was just thinking in the bathroom what would've happened if you had told me before, when we were younger. Even a week ago, before I met Antony."

That last part slipped out before I could catch it. I'm not even sure if I had realized that I was thinking it.

"What do you mean?"

I shrugged. "I don't know. I just wonder what I would've done."

"You would've went to the Elders," she said, matter-of-factly.

"Probably," I acknowledged.

"What about now," she asked softly.

I looked at her. "What do you mean?"

"What about now," she repeated, taking a step toward me, "now that you know your best friend has been in love with you for years?"

"I...we...I mean," I stammered and stuttered for a minute, trying to find the answer.

She pulled me to her and kissed me. I froze at first, but then, slowly, I kissed her back.

"What about now," she asked again.

"But, you have Louisa, and I'm with Antony. I-"

My words were cut off again by her lips on mine, this time strong and full of passion. I didn't resist. I kissed her back, wrapping my arms around her.

My mind was a fuzzy mess, like a TV station that had half of a picture but lots of static. I felt her hands move under my shirt, I felt her slipping it up over my head as I pulled the towel from her.

She pushed me down onto the couch, kissing down my neck, to my collar bone, to my breasts, to my stomach. Her hand slipped below my shorts and her fingers rubbed my wet heat before she pulled her hand out. I felt her fingers curl around the lip of my shorts and pull.

Part of me wanted this. Part of me was curious, and all of me was turned on. But the bigger part of me knew it was wrong. Not because she was a woman, in this moment that only served to heighten my passion. No, it was wrong because we were both with other people.

"Becca, we can't," I said, pushing her back from me gently.

She stopped immediately and stepped back. "I'm sorry."

"You have nothing to be sorry for," I said, putting my shirt back on. "I just can't-"

"What? Be with a woman? Because it seemed like you were just fine with it at first, and your body certainly seems to like it."

"No, it's not that," I said, trying to reach out to her.

She pulled away. "This was a mistake. I should have never done any of this, I'm sorry," she said, her voice breaking.

She pulled on her shorts and a top. "I'm going to go."

"Where? I thought we could spend the day finding a storage unit?"

"I can do that alone."

She was out of the door without another word. I was alone, in Antony's camper with no car and only deafening silence around me.

I sent a text before laying down to try to fall asleep, hoping that sleep would pass the time until Antony came home.

Me: I'm sorry, I just don't want to hurt Antony or Louisa.

I tossed the phone on the couch and went to the bedroom, laying in the bed crying.

I woke to the sound of tires on the gravel drive. A few minutes later Antony came inside with a bag of groceries.

"Hungry," he asked, before looking around. "Where's Rebecca?"

"She left. We had a disagreement."

He set the bag down and came over to me. "What happened?"

I wanted to tell him. I really did. But what good would come of telling him? At best he wouldn't be upset, but he would never trust me again. At worst, he would be angry and maybe even tell me to leave, and I definitely didn't have anywhere else to go right now.

"Nothing, she was just upset about everything. I guess we both still are, and we got on each other's nerves. Best friends do that I suppose."

"That they do. Just remember you're both going through things right now, so you can't be the only one that's being understanding and trying to help. She has to do her part too."

I nodded. "I'm sure we'll work it out."

"Good, because I've still got a truck full of her shit," he said with a smile.

I had forgotten all about her belongings that we had picked up the night before. I still needed to go to my house and pick up my stuff as well.

The idea of seeing my parents broke my heart. I was mad as hell at them, but that was still my mom and dad.

What I really needed was to feel them wrap me in their arms and tell me that they love me no matter what, that even if they don't agree with my choices, I'm still their baby girl.

But I knew that wasn't true. To them I was nothing. To them, I was just another sinner, destined to die.

"We should find a storage unit and drop off her stuff so we can get mine too."

"Give me a minute, I can get us one lined up. Probably get into it this afternoon."

"Okay, just make sure it doesn't cost a bunch, I need to watch my money."

He stood and smiled, grabbing his cordless phone. "I do the

landscaping for one in town, I'm sure it'll be cheap. And I can take care of it."

"No, I want to pay for it. I'm not going to mooch off of you more than I already am."

His smile grew. "It's not mooching, and besides, you'll pay me back when you get on your feet."

I knew he was just saying that, that if he got the unit he would pay for it and never take my money. But right now, I needed to be humble, so I just nodded.

A quick phone call later, and he was grabbing his keys. "Come on, let's go. We can drop her stuff off and when you have cell service you can call your parents and let them know you're coming to get your stuff."

The idea nauseated me, but I knew it was something that I had to do. So as soon as we had driven far enough for me to get a signal, I called my mom.

Of course, she didn't answer, so I left a quick message letting her know I would be there in a couple of hours to get my stuff. I texted her just to make sure she got it.

**Me: I'm coming with
Antony to get my clothes and stuff.
I'll be there this afternoon.**

My mother's response was
immediate, meaning that she had simply
ignored my call when I had tried.

Mom: Okay.

It didn't take long to unload the
bags and couple of totes of Rebecca's
at the storage unit. I wished she was
there, I wished that she wasn't mad at
me or hurt by me. But she was.

**Me: Hey, Antony got a
storage unit, dropped off ur stuff,
going to get mine now.**

I didn't know if that would make
her more upset or not, but she's the one
that left her stuff in my boyfriend's truck.
The ease with which my mind thought of
him as my boyfriend made me smile
despite myself.

He must have noticed my smile.
"What did she say? You guys better
now?"

I wish it was that simple. I wish we could just be 'better' and make everything normal again. But it wasn't.

"She didn't answer, I was actually just thinking about you," I said, taking his hand and holding it in my lap.

"Me? What about me?"

"Just the fact that you're my boyfriend."

The smile on his face when I said that was huge, and I couldn't help but feel my own smile return. Maybe everything would be okay after all.

***

It had only taken about a half hour to get from the storage unit to my house, my former house I reminded myself. I knocked on the door. My mother answered, and my anger and hurt melted for a moment.

She looked so weak. It had only been a couple of days since I had seen her, but she looked like she had aged a couple of years.

Her eyes were sunken deeply into her face, dark bags drooping under them. She looked like she had been crying, and a moment of gut-wrenching pain took me when I realized she had likely been crying over me.

"Mom," I said, and started to reach for her and hug her.

She backed away, eyes down. "Get your stuff and go."

My sadness and pain at knowing that I was hurting her was still there, but the anger flared, and I just took Antony's hand and walked past her and up the stairs to the attic.

When we got upstairs, Antony spoke as if he had been reading my mind.

"It's not your fault, you know."

Tears pricked at the corners of my eyes, and I brushed them away furiously with the back of my hand.

"No," I asked, sitting on the edge of my bed. My former bed, I reminded myself.

"How is it not? She had so much to deal with already, and I simply piled more onto her. How is it not my fault?"

Antony got on his knees and pulled me into him. I buried my face in his chest and let the tears free.

"It is not your fault, because it is not you that is shunning her. She is choosing not to speak to you. She is choosing to shun you. It is her own religious bigotry that is hurting her, not you."

I sobbed for a moment. If I had said that it was, in fact, me because I knew what would happen if I made the choices that I had, I would've fallen apart even more. Instead, I pulled back from him and wiped my eyes again.

"It doesn't matter. Right now, we just need to get my stuff and go."

We packed up my clothes in my luggage set that technically wasn't mine, but I didn't think my mother would stop me from using them.

I left all of the toiletries and shower stuffs where they were. I grabbed a few pictures, looked at my computer and decided I didn't need it for anything, and then turned to the stairs.

"I guess that's it."

Antony took my hand in his. "Sit here, I'll take the bags down and come back up."

Part of me wanted to leave with him right then, and part of me wanted to curl up in *my* bed in *my* room that I had slept in for so long and pretend that this was all some fucked up nightmare.

I had had plenty of those dreams, where my parents had made it through Armageddon, and I had not. Dreams where my memory was wiped from their mind and the only hurt that they felt was fleeting before I ceased to exist, even in the minds of those that once loved me.

But this was no dream. This was real. I had made, and continued to make, choices that made me happy. Even though my choices may make me happy, they brought pain to my family just the same.

I thought about what Antony said, that it was my parents' own bigotry that was hurting them and not me, but even so I couldn't help but feel like I was to blame.

"Do you have everything," my mother's frail voice asked.

At some point I must have laid down and I hadn't heard her come up the stairs.

"Mom, you shouldn't have climbed the stairs."

"Do you have everything," she just repeated.

"I think so."

My mother nodded. "Good. Then go. There is no need for you to call or text."

With that she turned and walked away. I stood and went down the stairs a moment later. As I walked out the door,

Antony standing next to the car, my mother put her hand on my arm. Her squeeze was so weak I barely felt it.

"Jehovah loves you. Don't ever forget that. It's not too late to fix your mistakes. It won't be easy, but if you rely on him, he will help you come back to us."

Had I known that that would be the last time I would see my mother alive, I would've said something. I would have hugged her, I would have held her, I would have told her that I loved her, I would have begged her to understand, to fight for her life.

But I didn't know that, and so instead, I simply walked out the door and didn't look back.

30

The next two weeks went by in a flash. I applied for, and got hired for, a job at Cedar Point in Sandusky, a temporary way to make money while I figured out a more permanent solution.

Rebecca had only texted me once, asking what the combination was for the storage unit where our belongings were. I had tried to text her, even call her, a couple of times with no answer.

Antony was working long days, taking advantage of the summer weather while he could. I wished that we could see more of each other, but the reality was we needed to make money to meet our goals. I needed to get a car, and he wanted to start his own business.

And so we worked long hours. I typically got home after him, and he always had a meal ready for me, even when he was asleep already, there was food in the fridge for me to rewarm.

We fell into a comfortable routine, taking advantage of every opportunity to spend time with each other. Usually, that time ended with us having sex, and my god was it getting even more incredible every time.

That night had been one of those times. That night when the fragile peace that we had built all began to crumble. I had a rare Saturday night off, and we had spent it watching a movie. Or at least, that was the plan.

His friend had burned a bootleg DVD of 'Pirates of the Caribbean: The Curse of the Black Pearl', and I couldn't wait to watch it. That was until we had cuddled up in bed and started it.

We hadn't made it past the opening scene when my hand drifted to his dick, stroking and teasing it. He pretended to ignore it for a couple of minutes, but then I felt his hand between my legs, and moments later I was on top of him, grinding us both to an orgasm.

Except the orgasm never came. It was almost nine o'clock and we never got visitors unannounced, but the sounds of tires on the gravel drive were unmistakable. I slipped off of him, and pulled on shorts and a top while he tossed on some sweats. No sooner had we dressed than there was a pounding on the door.

"I know you're fucking home," Rebecca hollered, her words slurring. "Come out here."

I looked at Antony. His face conveyed as much confusion as my own.

I opened the door and Rebecca stumbled back. Her eyes were red and puffy, she wore a tight, short skirt and a barely-there lacy black halter top. The smell of alcohol pouring off of her made my stomach turn.

"Did I interrupt something," she asked with a mirthless laugh.

"Becca, what's going on," I asked, walking towards her. "Did you drive like this?"

She laughed again and tossed her hands in the air. "Well, I had no one else to drive me. Louisa left me."

"What? What happened? Come in, let's get you some water."

I tried to take her arm, but she ripped it away from me.

"What happened," she practically yelled my words back at me. "I told her about us. That's what happened."

"Us," I asked, confused. "What about us?"

Rebecca slapped me. Hard. My head snapped to the side, and I saw

Antony coming down the steps from the trailer.

"Did you tell him," she asked, pointing at Antony. "Did you tell him how we kissed? How we almost fucked right there on his couch?"

I turned to Antony and saw his face had turned red. Anger? Embarrassment? I wasn't sure, but whatever it was it hurt me to see it.

"We didn't 'almost' fuck," I snapped, stepping right into her face.

"No? I guess I must have imagined taking your shirt off, you pulling my towel off, and us kissing while our bodies touched. Did I imagine how wet you were when I touched you?"

Somewhere in the back of my mind I heard the trailer door slam, but it barely registered.

"That was a mistake, and you know it. You're drunk, you're not thinking straight."

"I haven't been thinking straight since that day. I'm in love with you, Emily. I've been in love with you for a long time. I thought I loved Louisa, but she was just a body that I used to fill in because I couldn't have you. But you want me too, I know you do. Or at least you did that night," she said, putting her hand gently over where she had slapped me.

"I want to be with my boyfriend," I said, pushing her back. "I'm just figuring out my sexuality, but I care about him. You don't get to come here and try to fuck that up. You had years, fucking years, to be honest with me. You could have told me at any time how you felt. Who knows what would have happened? But no, you waited. You waited until my life was falling to shit, and I had one bright spot in it, and that made you jealous. So you tried to dim that light. Don't blame me because you are a fucking coward."

Rebecca just shook her head. "Yeah, I'm the coward."

When she turned and started to get in her car, I tried to stop her.

"Rebecca, you can't drive like this."

She didn't respond. She just started her car and sped away.

I turned to the camper just in time to see a now fully dressed Antony coming out of it.

"What are you doing," I asked, trying to grab his hand.

He yanked back from me and put his hands in the air. "Don't touch me, Emily."

He had brought his work truck home for the weekend, and he got in it and backed up.

"You can stay here, I'm leaving. The keys to the Hummer are on the counter if you need to go somewhere."

"Where are you going to go," I asked, fear, sadness, and an awful emptiness stabbing at me.

"It doesn't matter. Stay here as long as you need."

A moment later, he too was speeding off. I was left alone, and the loneliness I felt was maddening.

31

I spent the next two days mostly in bed. I only got out of bed to eat and use the restroom. Sleeping meant that I didn't have to think about all of the ways my life was fucked.

On the third day, I went to toss another frozen dinner in the microwave, only to realize there were no more. My options were bland cereal or some cans of vegetables that I found in the pantry.

I looked at my phone. It was almost noon, and I had no missed calls or texts. That wasn't surprising, my phone barely got a signal here, and no one wanted to talk to me anyway.

I took a quick shower, dressed in shorts and an oversized tee, and grabbed the keys to Antony's truck.

I drove into town and stopped at the oversized grocery store, Fuerst Mart, to get some supplies.

On my way into town, my phone had vibrated multiple times, but I had ignored it until I was stopped.

I parked and looked at my phone. Three voicemails and one text. The text was from an Elder at my old congregation, and when I checked the voicemails, two of them were from him as well.

Apparently, the Elders wanted to meet with me. I'm sure I would be disfellowshipped, but part of me wanted to meet with them just to let them know what I think about them. I'd have to consider my options.

Before I got out of the truck, I texted Antony.

Me: Had to run into town to get some groceries. Are you okay?

The third voicemail was from Cedar Point letting me know that my services were no longer needed. I hadn't even thought about my job, and was surprised to see that I didn't care that I had been fired.

I walked in the store and grabbed a cart, walking up and down the aisles blindly. It's not that I was distracted, it's that I wasn't focused on anything.

I felt numb. Occasionally I'd pass an item on the shelf, and my brain must have recognized it as something I wanted, and I would grab it and toss it in my cart.

I nearly jumped when my phone vibrated in my pocket.

**Antony: Not really, but
I'll survive.**

What the hell does that mean?
My thoughts went to all kinds of places:
had he lost his job? Was he in an
accident?

Then it dawned on me, he
probably meant he wasn't okay because
of us.

Us. That was a funny word. We
had been an 'us' for such a short time,
did we even count as an 'us'?

Me: I'm sorry.

His response was immediate.
Apparently he had been waiting for my
reply.

**Antony: Sorry that you
cheated or sorry that I found out?**

**Me: I didn't cheat. She
kissed me, and I shouldn't have let
her, but I am sorry.**

**Antony: She kissed you,
but you kissed back. You let yourself
get naked and she touched you in**

ways that I thought I was going to be
the only one touching you.

Me: Yeah, I did kiss her
back. But when she tried to take my
shorts off I stopped her. I didn't want
to cheat on you.

Antony: Oh, so she just
finger fucked you while you kept your
shorts on, huh?

Me: No, she did touch
me, but I pushed her off. It was a
mistake and I said I'm sorry.

Antony: Yeah, well, not
sorry enough to be honest with me. I
might not have even been that upset
if you'd have been honest. But you
chose to not tell me.

Me: So now what?

Antony: Idk. You can
stay there, I'll come back Saturday to
get some stuff.

Me: So you're breaking
up with me then?

Antony: Yes

Antony: No

**Antony: Idk. I guess we'll
need to talk. Saturday?**

Me: Yeah

Me: I'm sorry. I miss you.

That was it. He didn't give me a response after that and I went back to my shopping, but my mind was no longer void. The numbness was gone, and I was angry now.

Angry at myself, angry at Rebecca, and even angry at Antony for not understanding.

But why should he understand? In his eyes I had cheated, and I guess he wasn't wrong. But I stopped, I stopped after only a moment of weakness because I loved-

Holy shit. I was thinking that I loved him. My thought was that I had stopped what was happening with Rebecca because I 'loved him'.

I had never said that out loud, and I'm not sure I had even registered it internally until this moment. It hadn't even been a month, but I loved him as sure as I loved anyone.

Tears threatened my eyes, and I brushed them away quickly. I wasn't going to think about anything until Saturday. That's what I tried to convince myself anyway.

A few moments later, I was checking out and noticed a sign at the register: 'Join the team where you are 1st, Fuerst Mart!'.

I looked at the cashier for the first time. Had I even spoken to her when she started ringing my stuff?

"You guys are hiring?"

She smiled politely. "We are. You can get an application at Customer Service, right over there," she said, gesturing to the service desk.

I thanked her, paid, thanked her again, and then went over to get an application. The woman behind the counter handed me the two sheets of paper.

"Do you have any work experience," she asked with a smile.

"No," I lied, not thinking that the short stint I had at Cedar Point was worth mentioning.

"Oh, that's okay. My first job was here at Fuerst Mart as well! And now I'm the hiring manager, I'm just filling in for the service desk. What is your availability?"

That was the second time in less than five minutes that the first/Fuerst wordplay had been used, and it made me wonder if I was willing to put up with that for a paycheck. But, money wins.

"I'm available whenever. I don't have any other obligations right now."

The woman smiled even bigger. "How about overnights? I have a couple of positions open overnight, and that's always a great shift to make an impression and become a manager."

"I could do that, I'm sure."

"Okay, fill this out and bring it back," she said, sliding me an application. "Can you come Monday at 1PM for an interview?"

"Yeah, absolutely," I said, trying to sound excited. The truth is, I wasn't excited, but I did need a job.

"Sounds great! I'll see you then."

I thanked her, and left. Once I loaded my groceries' into Antony's truck I headed home.

Again, the thought was there before I had even realized that it was how I felt. It was home, but only because I shared it with Antony. I drove

there hoping that I wouldn't lose two
homes in less than a month.

32

I went home to put away the groceries. I hadn't gotten much and by the time that I had finished, I wasn't interested in food. I had been hungry an hour or so ago, but that changed when I had talked to Antony.

I tried not to think about how my whole world had changed in a very short amount of time, or the fact that Antony now *was* my world.

I tried not to think about what I would do if he couldn't forgive me for something that I would take back if I could. A meaningless kiss, a moment of weakness in my upside-down world.

I needed something to focus on, and I filled out the application that I had gotten at the market. At least doing this was something more productive than just going back to bed and trying to sleep my problems away.

It took me far longer than I would have liked to fill out the application. I stopped multiple times and got lost in my feelings.

Was I supposed to put down this address, Antony's address, as my home? Could I put Antony as my emergency contact like I had with Cedar Point?

It had been hard to leave my parents' house when they kicked me out, impossibly hard even, but at least I had an immediate solution then. What would I do if Antony decided I couldn't stay with him anymore?

In the end, I did put his, *my*, address. And I did put him down as my emergency contact. Fuck it. I could always change it later if I needed to, but for now I was going to think positively.

This would all work out, Antony and I would patch things up, Rebecca would come to her senses, and we would be friends again.

That last part gave me pause. Even if somehow Becca and I managed to figure out how to be friends again, what would Antony do? I didn't think that he would be okay with us being friends.

Was I willing to give up a friendship that I had had for years for him? Fuck. Everything was just so out of order right now.

That's because you turned your back on Jehovah! See? See what happens when you think you know better than him?

The voice in my head was my mother's, and I hated that it was there. But maybe it, she, was right. Maybe this was all punishment for the choices that I had made.

I was snapped out of my thoughts when Antony's phone rang. I had been here for almost a month, and I had never heard it ring except when he or Rebecca had called.

I picked it up without thinking.

"Babe?"

"Hi, is this Emily?"

I felt weak at the sound of the voice. Brother Weston, the Presiding Overseer of my congregation. Fuck. Why did I answer?

"Yes, may I ask who's calling," I said, feigning ignorance.

"Hi Emily, it's Brother Weston. I was hoping to catch you, I had left you a couple of voicemails, but I wasn't sure that you had gotten them."

"Oh. Yes, I just got them this afternoon actually. I haven't had a chance to call you back."

Nor would I have, I thought.

"That's okay, I'm sure you've been quite busy. I was just calling because we would like to meet with you to discuss some concerns that we have over things we've been hearing from your parents and some of the other Friends in the congregation."

"Concerns," I asked, feigning ignorance again.

Of course, they knew everything that my mother knew, and if there was any doubt that I was staying with Antony, that was gone the minute I answered his phone.

"Yes, concerns. I think it would be best if we discussed them in person though. Would you be available to come by the Kingdom Hall soon?"

Fucking Judicial Committee. Part of me wanted to tell him to fuck off, just go ahead and disfellowship me.

But part of me, a tiny, itsy-bitsy part, was thinking about that voice in my head. Maybe I should go, maybe I should beg forgiveness from Jehovah and let myself be punished.

"When would you like to meet?"

"Well, we can work with your schedule, but the sooner the better. Are you available this weekend?"

No. Fuck no. Antony was going to come back on Saturday, or so he had said, and voice or no voice telling me to meet with the elders, I'd be damned if I wasn't going to give him my undivided attention.

"No, this weekend won't work," I paused. "How about this evening?"

Now it was his turn to pause.

"Yes, I suppose we could do that. How does five o'clock at the Kingdom Hall sound?"

I glanced at the clock on the microwave. It was two-thirty.

"Can we do six? I have a few things yet to do."

"Six is fine. We'll see you there."

I didn't say goodbye, I just hung up. I looked over my application again, making sure that it was filled out completely. Then I got back in the truck and went to turn it in.

***

Back at Fuerst Mart, the same woman was behind the service desk. When she saw me approach, her big smile returned.

"Back so soon?"

I slid the application to her. "Yes, I had some other stops to make this evening and this was on my way so I wanted to drop it off."

"Excellent," she said, picking up the application. "Let's see."

"Like I said, I don't have any work experience, so I understand if you can't offer me a position-"

She waved her hand. "Nonsense," she said gently. "Like I said earlier, I think we are a great first job. When can you start?"

I was taken back by this. I hadn't expected to even talk to anyone today, I assumed that if they were interested, they would call and confirm Monday's interview. Now we were apparently going to skip the interview.

"I…well," I stammered. "I suppose as soon as you would like."

Somehow, the woman's smile grew even bigger.

"Excellent! I'm Amy," she said, extending her hand. "How does orientation on Monday sound?"

"That sounds great," I said, shaking her hand and smiling genuinely at her.

I had been worried about a job, and now that was one less worry.

"Perfect. I will see you at 10AM on Monday then."

I thanked her and left. My world was a little bit brighter with one stress removed from me. I had gone from having an interview on Monday, to having my first day.

But as I got in the car, my happiness faded slightly when I remembered that my next stop was to talk to the Elders.

33

I dreaded meeting with the elders the whole drive. There really wasn't a point, they knew what I was doing, and I knew they already had their mind made up about what they would do. I would be disfellowshipped.

Again, that little voice pricked at my mind and told me that maybe that was a good thing. Maybe everything that was going wrong in my life was a result of losing Jehovah's favor.

I parked and looked at the Kingdom Hall. I had grown up going to this building. I went there for meetings twice a week. I went to meet for field service at least double that. I had met Rebecca in this building. I had cried here, laughed here, and made what I thought were lifelong friends here. I had always imagined one day I would get married here.

I thought about how my dad used to say that churches were a 'house of the devil' and that when he walked into one, he could feel the evil presence of the demons that dwelled there.

I had taken that at face value when I was a child. But as I had gotten older, I had believed that maybe that was all in his mind. I remember going on a field trip in junior high to some of the historical sites in Cleveland. We had gone into a church that had been there for well over a century and was still in service. I didn't feel anything when I entered.

But now, sitting in this parking lot that I had sat in countless times, preparing to enter a building that I had entered countless times, I couldn't help but to feel that it was somehow evil. My skin crawled at the idea of walking through the doors.

I got out of my car and braced myself. I pulled the handle on the door and stepped in. It was eerily quiet, with no buzz and hum of the congregation. The lights were almost all dark, only the back row and the lights in the library, the dreaded 'back room' were on.

The feeling of horror that I imagined my father experienced walking into a church, I now felt walking into the Kingdom Hall. It was as if this building had been lurking, evil and ready to make my world crash down around me.

I pushed down the nauseating apprehension and walked into the library. Brother Weston, Brother Hornez, and Brother Steele all sat there talking quietly amongst themselves.

"Emily," Brother Weston said when I entered. "Thank you for coming, please, have a seat."

I sat and felt the weight of a thousand worlds on my shoulders. I felt like the room was pressing in on me, and I just wanted to run. This was not in any way what I had hoped for.

That small voice telling me that this might make things better was gone. The only voice remaining was telling me to get up and run away, and never set foot in this building again.

"Emily, first let me say that we've missed having you at the meetings recently. It's always a pleasure to have you here, and I know many of the Brothers and Sisters have missed you. I wish we were meeting under better circumstances."

I didn't know if he expected me to say something, he looked at me like he did, but I just looked back at him.

He cleared his throat. "Yes, well, it would be appropriate if we began this Judicial meeting with a word of prayer."

He started praying, and I didn't lower my head. I didn't close my eyes. I didn't do any of the things that were expected of me to do. I just looked at the three men, their heads bowed. Was one of these men the one that had raped Rebecca?

Fury coursed through me at the thought, and I pushed it down as he prattled on about 'learning what was in my heart' and 'helping your sheep find their way back into the fold' and whatever other bullshit it was he was saying.

It struck me as funny that a year ago I may have been moved by his prayer. I may have cried, thinking that this was my chance to repent and beg Jehovah for his forgiveness. But not now.

Now, all I saw was three old men deciding if I deserved to be in their cult or not. All I heard while he was praying was empty words, the way all of my prayers for my mother had turned out to be empty and meaningless.

"...in Jesus name we humbly come before you. Amen."

He finished the prayer and asked how I was doing.

"I'm sorry, did you call me here to make small talk?"

They had apparently expected a meek and humble sister, one that felt bad for the things she had done. What they got was a strong woman, one with bright, colorful hair, and cute makeup. Their shock at my response played clearly on their faces.

"No, we didn't," Brother Hornez stepped in. "But we do want to know how you are. The things that you are going through may be having an impact on the decisions you are making."

I thought about that for a moment. He was right.

"That's fair. I'd say the fact that my mother has gotten sicker and sicker, despite all of my prayers and the prayers of those in the congregation, the fact that she is willing to throw her life away rather than to take the medical care that might actually save that life, definitely has had an impact."

"Jehovah doesn't protect us from the sicknesses of this world," Brother Hornez said. "He can only promise that one day he will cure all ills and we will live in his paradise forever if we are loyal. Your mother knows that."

I just scoffed.

"Your mother has been loyal for so many years, would you see her throw that away now, stop fighting for Jehovah so close to the end?"

"I would see her fight for her life, if it was up to me."

Brother Steele nodded. "But that is what she is doing. She is fighting for her eternal life."

When I just shook my head, Brother Weston redirected the conversation.

"Your mother's trials are heartbreaking, to be sure. But we asked you to come here tonight to talk about you. Your mother told us a little of what she had witnessed, and also, we have heard that you are now living with a Brother from another congregation?"

I shrugged.

"Your mother says that she walked in on you masturbating, is that true?"

That coming from an old man, me being the only woman in a room with three old men, made my skin crawl. It was beyond creepy.

I shrugged. "That's what happened."

Brother Weston nodded. "And this Brother you're living with, have you had sexual relations with him?"

"I have," I said, looking him right in the eye.

"Who initiated the relations? Was it intercourse, or was it oral sex?"

If these old fucks thought that I was going to sit here and describe my sex life to them, they were about to be very disappointed.

"Does it matter?"

"Well, yes. We need to know the extent of the sin, so that we can determine what would be appropriate action to take."

"Are these the questions that an Elder asked Rebecca before he raped her?"

The question came out before I had even thought about it. But it was out now, and it had taken the room by surprise.

"We are aware of her accusations, but I can assure you, they were investigated and found to be without merit," Brother Weston said, recovering quickly.

I couldn't help but notice, however, that Brother Steele had turned dark red.

"Was it you," I asked, looking directly at him. "Do you like young girls?"

"Sister Marquette," Brother Weston said, "Please, let's stay focused on why we are here."

I ignored him. "Do you like taking advantage of children? I'm not a child anymore, but if I was, would you try to rape me too? Have you looked at me and wondered what I look like naked," I asked, leaning forward and squeezing my breasts.

"Sister Marquette! That is enough," Brother Weston nearly shouted.

"You're right, it is. Do you have a slip of paper and a pen by any chance? I'd like to write a statement."

Brother Hornez handed me a notebook and a pen.

I took them and began writing.

To whom it may concern,

I no longer wish to be a member of the Jehovah's Witness religion. Effective immediately, I request that my name be removed from active membership, and I not be contacted again by the organization.

Emily Marquette

"Short and sweet," I said, handing the notebook back to Brother Hornez. "You are all nothing more than self-righteous assholes that dare to sit there and judge me."

I stood and turned my back to them, giving a little wave without looking behind me.

"I'm going home to get fucked."

That wasn't entirely true. It would be nice, but I didn't know what was going to happen with Antony and I. They didn't need to know that though.

I got in my car and sent Antony a text.

Me: I disassociated myself.

A moment later I was driving out of the Kingdom Hall parking lot for the last time.

34

The entire drive home I thought about what my choice to leave the organization was going to do to my family.

I knew that my parents had already written me off, but I also knew that they held out hope that their shunning of me would make me come running back to their religion.

Now, with me making the conscious choice to abandon what they had taught me, what they had indoctrinated into me, they would be devastated.

But this was my life. And unfortunately for them, they didn't get to decide what I was going to do with my own life. I was happy for the first time in years, and I'll be damned if I was going to give that up.

Yes, right now things were kind of messy with my best friend. Yes, right now things were kind of messy with Antony. However the freedom and happiness that I had felt over the last couple of weeks was unlike any that I had experienced in the cult. And I had to believe that things would work out.

When I got back to Antony's trailer, his truck was parked out front. I parked, took a deep breath, and braced myself for an argument. We hadn't argued yet really, and I wasn't sure how he would handle it. Would he scream? Would he throw things?

I opened the door to the trailer, and he was sitting on the couch.

"Hi," I said, walking towards him.

He stood and backed away, into the kitchen.

"Do you love her," he asked, not even bothering to greet me.

What the fuck? Do I love her?

"As my best friend, yes of course."

"But you almost fucked her."

"I, we," I corrected, "made a mistake. Things are moving at a breakneck pace right now, and I am just trying to keep up. She admitted that she had been in love with me for a long time, she kissed me and I should've stopped her there."

"But you didn't."

I looked at him. "No. It got a little bit farther than that," I admitted.

"Why did you stop?"

"Because I love you," the words were out of my mouth before I could stop them.

"If you love me, then why did you kiss her at all?"

He didn't even acknowledge that this was the first time I had said that to him.

"Because," I said, becoming a bit irritated now, "like I said, everything is moving so fast, and that was too. It just happened, and I can't change it. But I didn't want her, I want you. I want to be with you."

"You want me to be with me."

He repeated my words as a statement, not a question, but I answered him anyways.

"Yes, I want to be with you," I said, closing the distance between us and touching his face.

He touched my hand, caressing it for just a moment, before he pulled it back from his face. The look in his eyes had changed. He had been looking hurt, almost lost. Now his look was nothing less than carnal.

He put my hand on his shorts. "Then get on your knees and prove it."

I knew that we should talk about things, not just do whatever it was that he was thinking. But I also wanted to feel him.

There was no doubt that this wasn't going to be love making. He may not even do the things that I had grown used to him doing for my pleasure. This was going to be him fucking me.

I dropped to my knees and undid his shorts, sliding them and his boxers down to his ankles and took his semi-hard dick in my mouth. It wasn't long before I felt him grow, and soon my mouth was full.

He put his hand on the back of my head and put his full length down my throat. I looked up at him, my eyes watering, and his look thrilled me. Not only was it carnal, but now it was also completely dominant.

The excitement that coursed through me at the thought of him using my body to satisfy whatever needs he was feeling sent a lightning bolt of pleasure to my core.

He pulled back from me, and I fought to catch my breath, working my already sore jaw. When I had had him in my mouth before, I had been in control, able to adjust however I needed to keep him from going too deep or keep my jaw from cramping.

He smiled at me, but I was again struck by the difference. It wasn't the loving, caring smile that I had come to crave. It was a smile of a man in full control.

"Catch your breath while you can," he said, releasing my head. "Go to the bed."

I stood and did what he ordered. I had watched some videos where the woman was dominated, and I had enjoyed watching them, but I always thought that I wouldn't want that. I now knew how wrong I had been.

He followed me into our bedroom and pulled my shirt off. I knew that my nipples were visibly hard through my bra, and a second later he had that off of me as well. He squeezed them both roughly, and I became weak at the pleasurable pain.

"Get on the bed, on all fours," he said, going to his small closet.

A second later he turned around, holding one of his neckties. Before I could even think to question why he had a tie, he was behind me, grabbing my arms.

My face hit the mattress as he pulled my arms behind my back. I felt the tie go around my wrists and tighten, though thankfully I realized not tight enough to hurt.

He pulled my shorts down to my knees, and slid two fingers inside of me.

"I see you're enjoying this too," he said, taking his fingers out and raising me by my bound arms. "Do you like how cunt tastes," he asked, shoving his fingers in my mouth.

I sucked his fingers, and he pulled them out of my mouth and let go of my arms, my face dropping back to the bed.

"I asked if you like the way cunt tastes," he said again, coming around front of me.

I didn't raise myself. I probably could have gotten onto my knees even with my arms bound behind me, but I knew that he wanted me like this. And in truth, I did too.

"I like how I taste," I said.

"Good, because I'm going to make sure you taste plenty of yourself."

He pulled me up by my hair and shoved his cock into my mouth again. I stretched and let him in my throat.

"Don't move," he said, as he grabbed a handful of hair with each hand and began thrusting deep and fast.

I watched his face as he took my mouth, my eyes blurry but locked on his. Hard, fast, and relentless he fucked my throat.

It didn't take long before he was moaning loud, and I could feel him twitching. With one last hard thrust, he held himself inside of me as I felt his load coating me.

He pulled out and let me go, this time my whole body fell flat on the mattress, and I gasped for air.

"Back on your knees," he ordered.

I tried, but failed, and he around the bed and got behind me. "On your knees," he repeated.

As I squirmed and tried to get back up, I felt his hand come down hard on my ass. The sting hurt so good. I gave a small whimper, and he laughed.

"Oh, did you like that," he asked as his hand came down again on my other cheek.

Before I could answer, he reached under my hips and pulled my ass up, and pushed my face into the bed.

"Don't move from that position," he said, leaving the bedroom.

The way I hated seeing him leave, and the way my body craved for him to come back and take me, was maddening.

A few moments later, he returned with a bottle of something in his hand. I couldn't make out what it was before he was behind me.

His arm wrapped under my hips again, and I felt another slap. And another. He spanked me over and over, my whimpers coming loud and fast. I wished I could see how red I must be, my cheeks felt like they were on fire.

He stopped and went to the closet again, grabbing another tie to bind my ankles, my shorts still around my knees.

A second later, his cock was inside of me with one thrust, making me cry out. The pure pleasure of feeling him stretching me had me wanting him in a way I hadn't known possible.

It was as if everything that we had done before this was foreplay, and this was the first time we were actually having sex.

I heard the top of the bottle snap open, and felt cold liquid running down my ass and over my hole. He rubbed the lube against my asshole with his thumb, massaging me as his cock throbbed inside my pussy.

"Oh god," I said, wanting so bad for him to push his thumb inside.

He pulled out and went to the pile of dirty laundry that was in the corner of the bedroom. Sorting through it, he grabbed one of my thongs and walked to his closet grabbing another necktie.

"Open your mouth," he said, standing in front of me.

I did, and he shoved my underwear in my mouth, wrapping the tie around my head and knotting it.

"Since you like the taste of cunt so much, enjoy that."

A second later, he was inside of me again. I felt more lube being dripped over my ass, and I was waiting eagerly for him to massage me again. He didn't.

My scream of pain when he shoved his full length in my asshole was muted by the thong in my mouth. He grabbed my wrists and pulled me up, his other hand wrapping around my chest and squeezing my nipple violently.

"Do you want me to stop," he growled in my ear.

Did I? I felt myself shaking my head before I even had registered the fact that I didn't want him to stop. I wanted him to use me, I wanted him to take whatever pleasure he could from my body.

Because I knew that I too was enjoying this. And I knew that if I did want him to stop, he would. He was exercising dominance, but I knew that he would stop immediately if I told him to.

"Good," he said, and let go of my wrists and my head fell back into the mattress.

I felt him pull out of my ass, and instantly slam back into me. It hurt, but nothing like the first time. He did it again, a little bit faster, until he was ravaging me.

My cries had turned to moans and I went limp, his hands gripping my hips as he took my ass.

Before I even realized it was happening, I came. I came more intensely then even when he had kept eating my pussy as I came over and over in his mouth.

He groaned and buried himself in me, holding his cock inside me, fingers digging into my hips, as I felt him come deep inside of me.

He untied my mouth and I spit out my underwear. After a few deep breaths he kissed me, hungry and full of passion. A second later he untied my hands and pushed me down on my back. He retied my hands, and then tied those to my ankle bindings.

"I'm almost done," he said, "but I'm not quite finished yet."

He left me there, my hands and feet above me awkwardly, and returned with my dildo. He slid it along the length of my wet slit, my hips pushing against it wishing he would put it inside of me.

"Do you want this," he asked, teasing me with the tip of my toy.

"Yes."

"Good," he said, before shoving its full length into my asshole.

I had expected it inside my pussy, and I cried out when he put it in me, stretching me even more than his cock had.

I cried out again when he drove himself inside of my other hole, my wetness taking him eagerly.

He pushed my legs back and began driving into me, over and over. My body responded, and I trembled.

I felt the orgasm building, the feeling of both of my holes filled at the same time was unlike anything I could have imagined.

Suddenly, he stopped thrusting, holding himself at the entrance of my sex.

"Are you ever going to let anyone touch you again?"

I hadn't expected the question, and I felt the orgasm slip away.

"No," I answered quietly.

He slammed himself in, and back out, stopping again when he barely touched me.

"Whose cunt is this," he asked, smacking his cock on my clit.

"Yours," I answered, quickly.

"I barely heard you," he said, bringing his hand down hard on my ass.

I felt myself tighten around the dildo that he had left inside of me.

"It's yours, only yours," I said, a little louder.

I loved the way it felt, him marking me as his. He wasn't controlling, he had never even begun to tell me what to do. But my body was something that he wasn't willing to share.

"That's a little better," he said, driving himself into me again. "Say it again."

"It's yours, baby, it's only yours," I cried out as he began fucking me again in earnest.

"Don't stop, repeat it."

"It's yours, my cunt is yours only and always."

As I told him over and over that my body was his, he drove himself faster and faster into me. I could feel the waves of an orgasm building, and I shouted louder and louder.

"Fuck your cunt," I told him, "come inside of it."

I felt my orgasm cresting just as he drove inside of me and held himself there. He pushed my bound legs back so far that it almost hurt, but that only caused me to come that much harder.

When he had finished, he pulled out of me, and then slowly pulled the toy out of my ass. He untied my bindings, and my legs and arms fell to the bed. I was exhausted.

He climbed on top of me, our naked bodies pressed gently together, and kissed me.

"I love you," he said with a smile.

35

The next day, he got up and had breakfast ready before I even awoke. In fact, it may have been the smell of the meats and eggs that roused me.

"That smells amazing," I said as I walked down the stairs in just my underwear and into the kitchen.

It wasn't lost on me that I was sore, very sore in fact, and the thoughts of last night sent heat coursing through me.

He looked up at me and smiled. "I hope it tastes as delicious as it smells."

He wiped his hands on a towel, looked me up and down before settling his eyes on my bare breasts, and closed the distance between us, giving me a quick kiss.

"Have a seat, let me make you a plate."

I sat, watching him move around his small kitchen. I knew that it was still early, and I knew that we had already faced more obstacles than most would in their first month or so of dating. But I really did love this man. And, according to him, he loved me too.

"You said you loved me."

The words had followed my thoughts and come out before I had realized that they were there.

He paused and looked at me.

"I do," he said, turning back to the plate he was making for me.

"Do you have plans today," he asked after he had set our plates on the table and sat down.

I shook my head as I grabbed a piece of bacon and ate it quickly.

"I thought maybe we could go to one of the islands, spend the day away from everything," he said, eating his breakfast with much more decorum than I.

I smiled. "I've never been, that sounds awesome."

He looked at me incredulously. "You lived in Northeast Ohio, and you've never been to the islands?"

I just shrugged. "I've never had much free time. Always something to do."

"Well, let's change that today. It's fucking awesome on the islands, and I love to spend as much time as I can on them. I haven't been in a while," he said excitedly. "Do you have a swimsuit?"

I did, but it was somewhere in the storage locker. "Probably in storage."

"Well, let's fix that. We'll go get you one before we head there."

"When did you want to go," I asked, glancing at the clock on his microwave. It was already after nine.

"As soon as you're ready."

"Let me just take a quick shower," I said, quickly finishing the rest of my food.

I stood and gave him a kiss on his cheek. "Thank you for breakfast."

***

An hour later, I stood outside of the changing room in the small mall boutique we had stopped at, Antony's eyes looking hungrily over me in the swimsuit I had chosen.

"Do you like it," I asked, already knowing he did.

"I love it," he said, standing up and smacking me on the ass gently. "Now let's get out of here so we can get to Kelly's."

I was excited to go to Kelly's Island. I had never really spent much time just doing nothing, and the idea of a relaxing day with him excited me.

After we paid, Antony led us to the bathrooms in the mall. "You should change into the bikini now, that way when we get to the island, you're ready to go."

I was wearing the shorts that I had gotten with Rebecca, and a tank top.

"I'll be right back," I said, heading toward the women's restroom with my bag.

"This way," he said, grabbing my hand and looking around. Satisfied that no one was watching, he pulled me into the family restroom and locked the door.

I smiled at him. "Wanted to watch me change?"

His hands were under my shirt in an instant, pulling it over my head. "I wanted," he said, releasing my bra, "to undress you."

His lips went to my nipples, and I moaned. "Stop before you get us kicked out."

He looked at me and pouted a pathetic pout, but he stepped back. I undid my shorts and let them fall to the ground, leaving me in just my lacy see-through thong. I turned so that my back was too him and slipped them down, bending over so that he got a full view of me.

"You tease," he said, coming up behind me as I stood.

I reached behind myself and grabbed him through his swim trunks.

"I bet if you can be quiet, you can probably have me before anyone knows we were even in here."

He needed no other prompting. His hand gently bending me over the sink as his other hand slid his shorts down. I gasped as he teased and played with my wet slit, his head going in before pulling out again.

"We don't have time-"

My words were cut off by a moan as he drove into me.

Ten minutes later, we were walking out of the mall. I felt a bit exposed in my bikini top and short shorts, but I couldn't help but to enjoy the stares that I got. I had spent my whole life covering my body, and to have it on display was exciting.

Antony noticed the stares as well, and slipped his arm around my waist.

"It's all yours," I whispered as his hand drifted down to my ass, slipping into my back pocket.

He smiled as he gave me a little squeeze and led me to his Hummer.

36

It was a perfect day as we parked and boarded the ferry to the island. The sun was warm with just a few puffy clouds in the sky, the water calm and smooth.

I curled into Antony and he held me while we made the trip. I had thought Antony would bring the truck, but he said it wasn't necessary, and I took his word for it.

After less than a half hour, the ferry was docking and we were getting off, hand in hand.

"What are we going to do," I asked.

Having never been to the islands, I didn't know what exactly there was to do.

"Are you hungry?"

"Not really," I said, laying my head against his arm as we walked.

"Then the first thing to do is going to be get a golf cart."

"A golf cart?"

"Uh-huh," he said, leading us to a storefront. "It's the easiest way to get around."

I was struck by how laid back the whole island had seemed so far.

Growing up, kids had made it sound like a party destination with lots of dancing and drinking. So far, it was chill, with not that many people our age.

"I thought it would be more of a party here."

He held the door to the cart rental shop. "Is that what you want? Because we can hit Put-In-Bay instead. They have more of the clubs and live bands and stuff."

I shook my head. "No, I want to see what you were excited about."

A few minutes later, he was driving the golf cart down the road, pointing out places that he liked to eat, or stories of things he had done with friends at this spot or that.

"You come here a lot?"

He shrugged. "Not anymore. Growing up, my dad used to bring us here. And then after he died I didn't come for a few years, but I spent a bunch of time here as a teenager."

I just held his hand and listened as he continued to tell stories. I loved hearing about his childhood, his life.

He pulled to a stop in a small parking area. "We're here," he said, hopping out of the cart and helping me out.

I looked around. "Where is here?"

"I'll show you."

He took my hand and led me down a path, and then up a set of stairs and onto a platform. I was shocked by what I saw. Huge cuts in the stone, hundreds of feet long and wide, they looked like strange dry stoney canals of some sort.

"What is this place?"

"Do you like it," he asked happily, as he stood behind me and pulled me to him, wrapping his arms around my stomach.

I put my hands over his and leaned into him. "It's amazing."

"This is one of the places that first made me question the organization. They teach that the earth is a little over six-thousand years old. But this," he said, wonder clear in his voice, "this is where glaciers cut through the rock over two million years ago."

"It's amazing," I said. "When was the first time you saw it?"

"I was eight. Dad had brought me here one weekend, he and my mom had been fighting and he wanted to go on a guy's trip, so he brought me here. We learned all about these grooves, and I remember saying that it couldn't be as old as they thought, because we knew the earth was only six-thousand years old."

"What did he say," I asked, lacing my fingers into his hands as he held me.

"He told me to always question everything. Looking back, I don't think he really believed in the Witnesses, I think he just went along for my mom's sake."

I wondered how I would've turned out, if I had a parent that had encouraged me to question things, to research things, instead of just following everything that the organization taught me.

"And did you?"

"Not at first," he sighed. "At first, I prayed to Jehovah that he would forgive my dad for doubting. I never told anyone what he had said, not even my mom."

"Why not?"

Antony waited for a long moment before he responded. I was afraid that I had hit a nerve, and that he would want to change the subject. I actually had hit a nerve, but he let me in.

"Because," he finally said, "by that time we knew that my dad was dying. I didn't want to do anything to get him in trouble. I thought that as long as he wasn't disfellowshipped, he would still get resurrected into the Paradise one day and I'd get to see him."

I turned to Antony, looking up at him. He didn't look at me, he just stared at the grooves, his eyes glistening.

"I'm sorry that you had to go through that."

He shrugged but didn't say anything. Whether he didn't trust his voice, or he didn't know what to say, I wasn't sure.

"No, really," I said, putting my hand on his cheek. "No child should have to think like that. You should've been able to just enjoy your time with him."

He leaned his head into my hand and closed his eyes. When he opened them, he smiled.

"Well, that wasn't the cards I was dealt. I'm glad even now, despite not believing in their paradise bullshit, that I didn't ever tell on him though. It would've only made his life worse."

"Eventually you questioned though," I asked.

I didn't want to hurt him with more memories, but I also wanted to know how he got to this point in his life. His journey wasn't the same as mine, and I wanted to know him.

"After he passed," Antony said, taking my hand and walking further along the viewing platform. "At his funeral, I couldn't get over the fact that they barely talked about my dad. He got maybe ten minutes, and then they spent an hour preaching about their shit. It wasn't a memorial of my dad. Hell, they didn't even really know my dad. And I was pissed off by that. That night I remembered what he said to me, 'question everything'. And so, I did."

"And that led you to not believing?"

"Yeah. But I couldn't tell my mom that. It would've broken her to know that I didn't believe."

I put my head down. "And now she's going to be broken by what we're doing."

He stopped walking and lifted my chin. "I'm an adult now. Dad has been gone for almost sixteen years. I've given her enough time serving this religion, this cult, that she wanted me to serve. It's time for me to live my life. I can't live to make her happy forever, it's my turn to be happy"

I was going to say something, though what I don't know. He kissed me, gently at first, and then passionately.

"And you make me happy," he said finally, "and I want to live my life with you."

37

We walked along the path back to the golf cart, my fingers laced in his. The silence between us wasn't uncomfortable. It was peaceful. Everything was so peaceful.

I couldn't think of the last time everything felt so right. Yeah, my parents hadn't spoken to me in nearly a month. Yeah, Rebecca hadn't returned my calls or texts in weeks. But, right now, in this moment, everything felt like it was just as it should be.

"You want to get some food," he asked, breaking our silence.

"I could eat."

"Fish okay? Theres a great restaurant here that serves fresh caught Lake Erie perch."

In truth, I had never had perch. We hadn't really eaten fish growing up.

"Sounds amazing," I said with a smile.

Everything felt so prefect today, that I was sure that lunch would be amazing.

A half-hour later, we were sitting down in the restaurant.

"What's the best thing to get," I asked, looking at the menu.

"I like the breaded perch and onion rings," he said, pointing to the spot on my menu. "But everything they serve is fantastic."

The waitress, a blonde about his age came and took our drink order, smiling a bit bigger at Antony when she turned to take his.

"She thinks your cute," I said playfully as she walked away, nudging him under the table with my foot.

He wrapped his ankle under mine, and brought my foot into his lap.

"Is she wrong?"

I gently slid my foot back and forth across his lap. "Not at all."

He blushed. That was the first time I had seen him do that.

"Are you okay," I practically giggled.

He cleared his throat. "Yes, but if you keep going like that, I won't be able to stand up any time soon."

I smiled but didn't stop, instead putting my other foot in his lap.

The waitress was back with our drinks. Sweet tea for Antony, and water with lime for me.

"Are we ready to order?"

Antony looked at me and I nodded.

"Ladies first," she said with a wink at me.

"I'll have the breaded perch and onion rings," I said, pointing to the same spot on the menu as Antony had a moment ago.

"Tartar sauce?"

"Yes, please," I said, closing the menu and handing it to her.

"And for you," she asked, turning to Antony.

"I'll do the same–"

His words hitched as I took the outline of his cock between my feet and rubbed it.

The waitress, to her credit, just smiled and took his menu.

"What the hell," he asked, a playful smile on his face.

"Tell me to stop," I said, smiling back.

He didn't. And I didn't.

I hadn't expected him to, but a few moments later, he looked me in the eye and I felt him twitch between my feet.

"Oh my god, really," I whispered.

He just kept looking at me hungrily. I glance around. The only other people in the restaurant were behind me, several tables away.

It was a good thing that we were in between the lunch and dinner rushes. I pulled one side of my top away and squeezed my nipple, before putting it back into place.

"Fuck," he moaned out quietly.

I took my feet from his lap and laughed. I loved the power I had over him, my ability to drive him wild.

As the waitress approached with a tray, he picked up his glass of tea and fumbled it, spilling the contents onto his swim shorts.

"Oh my god, are you okay," the waitress asked, placing the tray at the empty table next to us and grabbing the towel on her apron.

I felt a surge of jealousy when she took the towel and began dabbing it on his shorts. I also felt a strange twinge of…pleasure? There was something sexy about another woman touching him where I had just made him come.

"I can get that, thank you," he said curtly, taking the towel from her hands.

She turned as red as I had ever seen anyone turn.

"Of course, I'm so sorry, let me get you more napkins," she said and scurried back towards the counter.

A very red-faced Antony stood and went to the restroom. When the waitress came back, she apologized profusely.

"I'm sorry, I don't know what I was thinking."

I smiled. "It's fine, thank you," I said.

Was it fine? As she put the food on the table and walked away, the image of her with Antony in her mouth popped into my head. A shot of electricity went through me.

What the hell? I tried to tell myself that I didn't want to ever see Antony with anyone but me, but even as I was thinking that, images of him doing all sorts of things to her while I kissed him, and her, and…

My thoughts were cut off by Antony's return.

"You okay," I half giggled.

He blushed again. "Yeah, I'm fine. Sorry about that."

I cocked my head to the side. "Why are you sorry?"

"I should…I mean…she…" he stuttered and stammered.

I just smiled as I looked at him, his face red and panicky as he looked down.

"Did you enjoy her touching you?"

His eyes snapped to mine.

"What? No, it wasn't…I didn't…"

I reached out and took his hand. "Babe, it's okay."

He looked at me for a second. "Babe?"

I shrugged. "If you don't like it, I can call you something else."

He laced his fingers in mine. "No, I like it. You've just never called me that before."

I leaned across the table and got close to his ear. "Well, *babe*, did you like having another woman touch your cock right after I made you come," I asked in a husky whisper.

I expected more stuttering, so I was shocked when he whispered back. "And if I say yes?"

A rush of excitement ran through me. Heat bloomed where it shouldn't at the idea of another woman touching my boyfriend. But it did. I pulled my face back.

"When are we going home," I asked quietly.

He looked saddened by my question. As if the day was ruined, and I just wanted to go home. As if he had answered wrong.

"I had thought that we could stay here tonight, my uncle has a camping lot that he leases all summer, and they have supplies and everything at the office. But, if you want to go home…"

His voice trailed off, and I stood and came to his side of the booth. He scooted over to make room for me, and I slid my hand to his shorts again.

"Did you," I squeezed him a little, "like being touched," I slid my hand down a little lower, "by another woman?"

I squeezed to the point where I hoped it would be on the edge of painful and pleasurable. He gasped and looked at me.

"Yes."

One word. One word, complete honesty, no bullshit stammering, no telling me what he thought I wanted to hear. Jealousy and lust battled again in my mind.

In truth, I didn't know *what* I liked, what I wanted, who I was sexually. I had masturbated to all different kinds of porn, guys, girls, groups. Hell, depending on the mood I was in, I would search out videos of a woman being tied up and used like a toy over and over by a whole group of men.

It all had excited me, it all had given me fantasies. But that was when I was single. What about now? What about now that I had a boyfriend?

And then there was the kiss with Rebecca. It had done so much damage to our friendship, maybe destroyed it, and it had hurt Antony. But I almost didn't stop it. I almost didn't stop her. And the way he had angry fucked me after, the pure use of my body for his pleasure…

"Emily?"

I realized that my hand was still on him, though I wasn't squeezing him anymore. He looked at me as if I was in another world. How many times had he called my name?

"Sorry, I was just thinking," I said.

That was when I realized that our waitress had come back. I'm guessing she had asked us if we wanted dessert, but given that I was completely lost in my own thoughts, I had no idea. I looked at her and quickly removed my hand from Antony when I saw her staring at it.

"I'll come back," she mumbled, and left us.

I looked at Antony and laughed. His mind had to be absolutely racing, and the look on his face was one of horror at the waitress having seen what I was doing.

"You don't think she heard what I said, do you?"

He just shook his head.

"Okay. Give me your card," I said, holding my hand out to him.

He reached into the pocket of his swim shorts and pulled out his bank card.

"I'll go pay, you go outside and wait for me."

I gave him a quick kiss, and walked what I hoped was sexily over to the counter.

38

Fifteen minutes later we were driving to the campsite. Antony stopped at a small building while I waited in the car. Thoughts of the waitress were swimming through my head, thoughts of her and Antony. Thoughts of kissing him after he had made her come, her taste on his lips.

My mind leapt to thoughts of Rebecca, of our kiss, and our almost… whatever that was going to be.

I pulled out my phone. I had texted and called her time and again after that day, but I had never gotten a response.

Me: Hey. I miss you.

Antony had been angry at me, so angry, for what had happened. But she was my best friend. And I couldn't help but miss her. We had talked every day for years and this not talking for weeks was driving me crazy. I had done a fair job at blocking it out, but it crept up when I least expected it.

I hadn't realized that Antony had returned, a small wagon full of a tent and firewood in tow.

"Are you okay," he asked, as he opened my door and looked at me worriedly.

It was only then that I realized my eyes were blurry. I hadn't been crying, but clearly my eyes were close to bursting. I scrubbed at them quickly.

"I'm fine," I said, slipping out of the golf cart to help him load the supplies.

He took my face in his hands. "What's wrong?"

My best friend won't talk to me, you hate her, and I can't speak to my family. In the end, I went with that.

"I just miss my mom, I guess."

He pulled me into a hug and kissed the top of my head.

"I'm sorry. It's disgusting what that organization makes people do to their own family."

I just shrugged. "Let's just enjoy our evening, shall we?"

He let me go and smiled. "Yes, lets. I've got plenty of wood-"

"Yeah you do," I cut him off with a smirk.

He just smiled and continued.

"and there is stuff in there for s'mores as well. We can get set up and then go get some dinner later before everything closes if you get hungry."

I started to grab some of the stuff to help him load it, but he stopped me.

"I've got it, just hop in and relax."

A few minutes later, he returned the wagon, and we were on our way. I glanced at my phone. Rebecca hadn't responded. I didn't really expect her to, but I still had hoped she would.

"Have you tried calling," he asked, glancing at the phone in my hand.

I pushed the phone into my pocket. "No, not lately. They don't want to talk."

He just nodded and drove.

The campsite was gorgeous, trees lined three sides and there was a small beach across from the dirt path that we took to get to it. I assumed that there must be other sites around, but from ours you couldn't see them.

I had never been camping, but the idea was exciting to me. I always loved the outdoors, and while my parents had never shared that love I was quietly glad now that they didn't. It was nice to experience this for the first time with Antony, with the man I loved.

I offered to help him set up the tent, but he told me it was no problem, and that I could just relax. That was my plan.

My plan lasted all of about a half hour. I took a quick walk over to the beach and listened to the waves. A few jet skis and a boat passed in the distance, their engines drowned out by the sounds of the lake lapping at the shore.

I took my shorts off and waded into the water. It felt cool at first, but soon it was perfect with the heat of the late evening sun beaming down. I closed my eyes and floated for a moment.

"How's the water," Antony's voice came from the shore.

I opened my eyes and righted myself. He stood there in just his swim trunks, still stained with the tea that he had spilled on them.

"It's perfect after a second. Come in?"

He shook his head. "Maybe later, I want to finish-"

He stopped talking when I undid my swim top and bobbed up out of the water so he could see my breasts.

"I mean, the tent is basically up," he said with a smile, wading in towards me.

I swam towards the shore until I was in waist deep water. When he got close, I turned to swim away from him. He grabbed me by my ankles and pulled himself between my legs, his bulge pressing against my ass. He reached a hand under my chest and pulled me up tight to him.

"Brother Householder, what are you doing," I practically whispered, feigning innocence.

His husky growl came as he pinched my nipple between his fingers. "Preparing to fuck you."

I turned myself to face him. "And how are you going to do that with our bathing suits on?"

He untied his trunks, slipping them off and tossing them to the shore. I wrapped my hand around him and stroked gently.

"What about mine," I whispered into his ear.

He slid a finger under my bottom and between my lips, finding me slick with need.

"I don't need to take them off," he said.

I wrapped my legs around him, and felt him slide my bathing suit over. A second later he drove himself into me. I kissed him with all of the passion I had ever kissed with, our tongues fighting furiously with each other.

His mouth moved to my neck, to that spot right on my collar bone that drove me wild. I felt him pull my skin into his mouth hungrily, his hands sliding under my bathing suit and gripping my ass. When I began grinding against him, I felt his teeth dig in just a little to my neck.

"You feel so perfect," I moaned in his ear.

"You do," he said.

He spun towards the shore and began walking out of the water. He carried me like I was weightless in his arms, never removing himself from me. He carried me across the dirt road and to our campsite, setting me down on the grass gently.

Never taking himself from me, he began thrusting, hard and fast. I dug my nails into his back as he pushed me towards my orgasm. Having sex outdoors where someone might see was invigorating.

I began moaning, softly at first, then louder and louder.

"Harder. Don't stop, please don't fucking stop," I begged.

He pinned my legs back and drove himself into me, slowing down but driving so deep he bottomed out. I screamed with pleasure as the heat of the orgasm poured out of me. He threw his head back and moaned, one last deep thrust before he exploded inside of me.

That was when we heard a cough from the road.

"What the fuck," Antony said, jumping up and trying to cover himself.

He'd left his swim trunks on the beach and looked somewhat comical trying to hide himself with his hands.

At the edge of the road stood Ashley, the waitress from the restaurant we had ate at only a few hours earlier. The sun was starting to set, and she was bathed in an orange glow.

I didn't get up or try to cover myself. He had never taken my swim bottoms off, but I lay there, spread eagle with my breasts exposed, nipples hard from the sex and the cooling air.

"You made it," I smiled.

She walked towards us and smiled back. "And just in time it would seem."

"What the fuck is going on," Antony asked.

He had covered himself with a towel and was looking between Ashley and me.

"She said that you liked it when my hand was on you earlier. She invited me to come keep you guys' company tonight," Ashley said with a devilish smile and a shrug.

She had changed from her uniform and wore shorts that were even shorter than my own, and a pink tube top that strained to hold her in.

"You what," he asked, turning to look at me incredulously.

I finally stood, walking over to him and kissing him.

"It turns out, I liked her hand on you too."

"I…but…we," Antony stammered.

Ashley walked toward us, pulling her top over her head, and tossing it where I had just laid as she closed the distance.

"I can leave, if you don't want me here."

I looked at Antony, his eyes glued to her chest, and his stiffness clearly visible again under his towel. I pulled the towel off and took him in my hand.

"I feel like he wants you here," I said, dropping to my knees and licking the side of his dick.

Ashley came over and got down on the other side of him, copying my movements before taking all of him in her mouth with a moan.

Antony looked at me, desire warring with apprehension.

"Oh fuck," he finally said, tipping his head up.

I stroked Ashley's hair as she expertly sucked my boyfriend. I knew that he enjoyed it when I sucked him, but she was licking and twisting and stroking in ways that I had never done. I stood and kissed Antony.

"Does her mouth feel good wrapped around you," I whispered in his ear.

He just put his hand behind my neck and pulled me into a passionate, hungry kiss.

As he started to moan harder, Ashley pulled away from him. She stood and walked over to where he and I had just been.

"You come after I do," she said, smiling at Antony.

As she lay back on the grass and slipped her shorts off, nothing underneath I was excited to see, he walked over to her, and got down in front of her. While I shaved clean, she left just a small patch of hair at the top of her triangle. The way it looked drove me wild and made me wonder if I should try that.

He wrapped his arms around her thighs and buried his face between them. I joined them, kneeling next to Antony and pushing his hips up from the ground enough to take him in my hand. I stroked him, but my eyes were on the naked woman he was pleasuring.

Desire coursed through me, and I wanted so badly to taste her too. I wanted to be touching her breasts, sucking on her nipples, instead of stroking him. But I had promised him that my body was only his, and I wouldn't break that promise.

"Kiss me," Ashely begged me, lust in her eyes. It was as if she had read my mind.

"I told you at the restaurant," I said with a soft smile, "you only get him."

Antony took his mouth from her and turned his head to me. "We can share," was all he said before he returned his mouth to its task.

I didn't need to be told twice. I went up to her, tucked a lock of hair behind her ear, and kissed her.

Gently, full of soft passion, our tongues danced and stroked each other. My hand slid down her chest to her nipple and I teased it. She broke the kiss and gasped.

I kissed her lips one more time, before taking her breast in my mouth. She moaned and bucked hard against Antony's face as I ran my tongue over her nipple. When I teased it gently with my teeth, she screamed out and came.

Antony got to his knees, and I kissed him. Fuck she tasted even better on his lips than I did. He slid his body the length of her, and teased her with his cock.

"I brought condoms," she said, "in my shorts."

I went and got them; she had brought at least a dozen. Wow, she must have really planned on making a night out of this. The idea excited me and I hurried back.

I dropped to my knees in front of Antony and took his cock in my mouth. He was hard, so fucking hard, and part of me wanted to just suck him until he came. Instead, I pulled back and slipped the condom on.

"Fuck her," I whispered in his ear.

He slid back into position on top of her, and she looked at me as his cock went inside of her. I was jealous. Jealous of both of them.

I wanted to be her, getting fucked by my boyfriend. And I wanted to be him, fucking her. The jealousy drove me wild, and I took off my bottoms.

As he drove into her, her breasts bouncing up and down with each thrust, I came up to her and kissed her.

"Let me taste you," she said, her voice deliciously husky.

Antony got onto his knees and pulled her to him, never stopping his thrusts. I faced him and lowered myself down over her. As her tongue, soft and gentle, licked the length of my slit, I closed my eyes.

I moaned loudly when she pulled me closer to her, tongue teasing my clit. On, and then off, and then on again. I set my weight down slowly on her face, and she stopped teasing.

My eyes opened as she began eating me, the heat between my legs growing when I locked eyes with Antony and saw his smile. He's enjoying this, all of this, and so am I.

I looked down and watched as his cock drove in and out of Ashley, his length appearing almost in full before disappearing again with each thrust.

I pulled his face to mine, and somewhere in the back of my mind I was impressed that he didn't lose his rhythm.

"Are you enjoying fucking her?"

He nipped at my ear before he whispered back. "Every second of it."

He pulled his face back, and I could see the look in his eyes. That look that he gets right before…yes, there it is. His abs went taught and he drove fully into her, holding himself deep inside of her as he looked me in the eye and came.

When he pulled out, I turned myself back around, letting Ashley catch her breath for a moment.

"Kiss her."

He obeyed, kissing her deep and long.

"Do I taste good on her lips," I asked, rubbing my clit.

Antony brought his mouth to mine and kissed me. Oh fuck, I do taste good.

"Kiss her and see," he said, moving himself out of the way.

I kissed her, and it wasn't as passionate as the kiss they just shared. It was tender, and soft, and I fucking tasted amazing.

Ashely looked at Antony as our lips part.

"Watch as I make your girlfriend come."

It didn't take long, her mouth on my heat, Antony's on my breasts, before I was coming. I screamed out as I did, louder and more passionate than I had ever imagined doing, and she didn't stop until I pushed her away.

Ashley slid up beside me, her mouth glistening with my wetness, curling next to me in the grass.

She licked her lips as she gently traced my curves, fingertip moving from my lips, slowly down to my nipples, barely touching me as she circles my clit, and I shivered.

The sun had disappeared beyond the edge of Lake Erie, and the sky was almost dark.

"I should start a fire and finish the tent," Antony says, starting to head across the road to get his swim trunks.

"You don't need shorts to do that," I giggle out.

Ashley added her agreement to my statement, and he just shook his head with a smile. Soon, flames filled the fire pit, and he was putting the last of the tent together.

"Is this your guys first time sharing," Ashley asked, her fingers still dancing across my skin.

I nodded. "Actually, we've only been going out for a little over a month. We were both raised in a cult, and sex is new to us."

This seemed to surprise her, and her hand paused on my stomach. Her brown eyes had flecks of honey in the light of the crackling fire, and I wanted so badly to kiss her again. To feel her tongue in my mouth before it was sucking on my clit.

"You could have fooled me," she said with a smile that reached her eyes. "Well, not the first-time sharing part, but neither of you seem like you've only been having sex for a month."

I smiled back, heat rushing between my legs. "We're not bad, huh?"

She tipped her head to my chest and licked my nipple quickly, teasingly, before pulling back to look at me.

"You both are incredible. If you decide to keep opening things up, there will be some lucky people getting to have fun with you."

I propped myself onto my elbow and kissed her. God, I didn't want the night to end.

"Tent's done," Antony said, coming and laying on my other side.

Ashley broke the kiss, and climbed on top of me, her wetness slick on my stomach as she leaned over and kissed Antony.

In that moment, I realized that the jealousy was gone. He was kissing another woman, he just fucked another woman, but I wasn't jealous. I was excited.

We were having an amazing night, but tomorrow night, it would be me that cuddled up to him in bed. And the night after that, and the night after that.

Sex and love are two very different things, and I couldn't help but think of how I would have never known any of this if we'd stayed in the cult.

"You know," Ashley said, looking at me, taking my breasts in her hands, "she was very generous to offer to share you."

I smiled at her before Antony kissed me. "Yes, she was."

"So," she said, turning to Antony, "are you going to let her bring a man in next time?"

I hadn't even thought about that, but now my mind raced through the possibility of it.

I thought about last night when he had tied me up and fucked me. He had shoved my dildo in my ass and left it there as he buried himself in me. The feeling of him and the toy drove me wild. What would two cocks inside of me at the same time feel like?

He smiled. "I don't know," he said, coming down to my ear and whispering, "do you want another cock inside of you?"

He had been honest when I asked him if he liked Ashley's hand on him at the restaurant. I would be honest in return now.

"I want yours," I said, taking his hardening sex into my hand, "in my pussy, and someone else's in my ass, both fucking me until I scream."

I felt his cock twitch and his breath catch as he just smiled back.

"Well, for now, you'll have to settle for my mouth," Ashley said, as she slid down my body and put her lips on mine, tongue dancing across my clit.

I moaned and closed my eyes, back arching as I began to move my hips up and down on her face.

I felt Antony move from my side, and I looked down as he got behind her. Her eyes never left mine as the sound of a condom wrapper ripping open came and he began thrusting inside of her, her moans vibrating against me and pushing me closer to an orgasm.

Watching Antony grab her hips and drive himself deep and fast into her, no love just primal lust, drove me over the edge.

I started calling out Ashley's name, begging her not to stop. She moaned deeply, her mouth like a vibrator as her tongue never left my clit.

Finally I came, grabbing her head and driving my hips against her, and she wrapped her arms around my legs and pulled me in until my body stopped shaking with the power of my orgasm.

I finally pushed back a little, and watched the incredibly sexy scene of Antony fucking her. Both of their eyes were on mine, but she closed hers and let out a moan when Antony grabbed a fistful of her hair and pulled her head back a little.

I'm not sure what came over me, but I stood and walked over behind her, kissing Antony as I ran my hand over her ass. I smacked it hard, and she let out a small whimper of pleasure.

"Do you like the way my boyfriend feels inside of you," I asked, smacking her again.

"Yes," she moaned out, "oh fuck yes."

I slid my hand between her cheeks, Antony's cock driving in and out of her, and put pressure on her empty hole.

"Oh, please, play with me," she begged.

"Spit on it," I said to Antony, and he obliged.

I massaged the saliva around her ass and slipped my finger in, slow but steady. Ashley's moans grew louder, and I slid my finger back out.

"Again," I said to Antony.

I slipped two fingers in her this time, massaging and rubbing her, watching her stretch around my digits.

I took my fingers out and went up to face her. "Do you want to feel him come in your ass," I whispered, running my wet fingers over her lips.

She just bit her lip and nodded before Antony drove into her and made her close her eyes again.

I walked back to Antony, and ran my hand down his stomach, pushing against him to stop him from his thrusting.

He pulled out, looking confused by me stopping him. I quickly took the condom off.

I got on my knees and took him in my mouth for a brief moment. I turned and buried my tongue in Ashley, licking and twisting around her as much as I could. She pushed against me, begging for more.

"Finish in her ass," I said with a smile, before I lay my head down under her legs.

I pulled her to me, and as my tongue met her clit, I heard her gasp at Antony's cock being slowly pushed into her.

It didn't take long for him to come, her tight ass milking his throbbing cock. When he pulled out, I wrapped my arms around her waist and pulled all of her down on me, feeling her lips quiver as her own orgasm took her. She cried out as her body shook, and then I let her go and she rolled off of me, her body going limp in the grass next to me.

40

We invited Ashley to stay the night with us, the tent that Antony had slept six people so there was more than enough room. She declined, apparently she had a husband to get home to, and left a few minutes after we had finished having sex.

I hadn't asked her if she was in a relationship, and in the end I didn't really care. Antony, however, seemed to care.

"I wish I'd have known she was married," he said with a sigh, dropping down next to me in the tent.

I cocked my head and looked at him. "Why?"

Antony shrugged. "I don't know, it just feels wrong."

I touched his face. "We don't know anything about her. For all we know, they have an open relationship. She may go home and tell him about the mind-blowing dick she just got from the most handsome guy on the planet."

That made him smile. "Maybe," he said, turning to me. "You think I'm the most handsome guy on the planet?"

I nodded. "Uh-huh. And don't forget the mind-blowing dick," I said, smiling back at him as I ran my hand down his abs and lower.

He groaned. "Don't get me started again, because I will go all night, and I'm exhausted."

I did get him started, however. "Lay down and let me do the work."

I rode him until I felt his come deep inside of me, and then I curled next to him, and we fell asleep in each other's arms, exhausted and satisfied.

***

The next morning, I woke to Antony running his finger gently over the side of my body. Down my shoulder, across the side of my breast, slowing on my hip before cupping my ass with his hand.

I moaned softly. "What time is it?"

He grabbed his phone. "Almost seven."

I snuggled in closer to him. "Mmmm, let's just lay here for a few more minutes. I have to go to orientation at ten."

He slipped his arm under my neck and pulled me close to him. His body still smelled lightly of Ashley's perfume, and heat burned between my legs at the memory of her.

I was unsure if I was going to enjoy what I wanted us to do when I invited her, but now, after it was done and she was gone, I wanted it again.

"Last night was amazing," I said into his chest.

"Yeah, it was," he said, stroking my hair.

There was something off about how he said it. I pulled back from his chest enough to look at him.

"What's wrong?"

He shook his head. "Nothing."

"No," I said, sitting up, "not nothing. Something's wrong, and we won't last very long if we aren't open about things."

He sighed. "I just... I don't know. Last night was amazing," he started.

"But?"

"But I can't help but think that maybe I won't keep you satisfied. I enjoyed every moment of last night, but if we never do anything like that again, I'll be happy with only having you."

"And you think I can't be happy with only having you too?"

He shrugged. "I don't know. You said you wanted to have another guy with us. And the way you enjoyed yourself with Ashley…I don't know, I just worry that you'll want things that I can't give you I guess."

I slid on top of him and kissed him. "I want you. I want to be with you, I want to sleep with you, I want to build a future with you. If you aren't comfortable with other people sharing our bed for a few hours, then last night was a one-time thing. I don't need anything other than you."

Even as I said it, I wasn't sure I believed it. Before last night, maybe. But after last night, after the raw pleasure of watching him with another woman, of tasting that woman and being tasted by her, the truth was that I wasn't sure that I could be happy with just him.

Sex was so much better than I could have ever imagined, and I craved it, but not just from him. I wanted a woman's touch again. And, yes, I absolutely needed to feel what it was like to have two cocks inside of me at once.

"Good," he said, kissing me back before running his hands across my body.

His hand found its way between my legs, and I shuddered gently. "I think we have time for this before we have to go," I said, taking his dick in my hand and sliding myself down onto him.

An hour later, we had returned the tent, and the golf cart, and were standing hand-in-hand waiting on the ferry.

"I love you, Emily," he said without looking at me.

"I love you too," I said, resting my head onto his arm.

The rest of the time between the ferry and his truck, we didn't talk. We just held onto each other. I loved the way it felt with his hand in mine, or his arm around me. Words weren't necessary.

Everything felt right, felt comfortable, between us. I felt happy. Truly, deeply happy, in a way that I hadn't felt in a very long time, if ever at all.

When we started driving back home, his phone rang. I let go of his hand as he spoke on it, some sort of business thing it sounded like.

"What was that about," I asked when he ended the call.

"I was telling my uncle how I didn't really want to do snow removal this year, that I wanted to find a way to keep doing landscaping. He put me in touch with one of the crews that he used when he built his house in New Mexico. I didn't think anything was going to come of it, but they offered me a position for the winter."

"In New Mexico," I asked.

Why hadn't he said anything to me about this before?

He must have picked up on my irritation because he quickly apologized.

"Yeah, I'm sorry I didn't tell you, but I really didn't think it was going to happen."

"When did you first talk to them?"

He sighed. "After our fight about Rebecca. I crashed at his house, and we were talking. He gave me their number and I reached out, but like I said, I didn't think it was going to happen, so I didn't want to bug you with it."

"But it is happening," I said flatly.

"Yeah, they offered it to me, but it's no big deal, I don't have to go."

Was I annoyed with him for not talking to me about it? Sure. Was I going to stand in the way, even a little, of him working towards his goals of owning his own company? Fuck no.

"When?"

"It would be from October through March. The owner has casita that he said I could rent while I'm there."

"And you want to do it?"

He shrugged. "The pay would be really good, and I could learn about desert landscaping too, so that could be useful. It was just an option, I didn't…"

When his voice trailed off, I finished. "You didn't know if we were going to be together anyway."

He sighed. "It sounds silly when you say it. I knew I loved you, so of course we'd be together. But yeah. I was mad at the time, and I guess I was just thinking what if. But I'll tell them I can't, it's okay. There's money to be made in snow removal too."

I took his hand. "No, you won't pass up this opportunity. What about me?"

"You could come if you want, or if not you could stay in the camper. If you didn't come, I could catch a flight back as often as possible to see you. It doesn't cost much to fly from there to Cleveland."

I laced my fingers with his. "Well you're going to accept the offer. Period. We'll figure out the rest. It's only August, so we have some time."

**He pulled our hands to his lips
and kissed mine. "I love you."**

41

I sat through the world's most boring orientation at Fuerst Mart, trying to keep from falling asleep or letting my mind wander back to last night.

My group had only three people in it, myself, an older guy named Gus, and a young woman about my age named Jane. Gus was going to be a day shift cashier, but Jane would be with me on the overnight stocking team.

The lady leading our orientation, Michelle, droned on, then would break for us to watch a video about the company, and then drone on some more. I couldn't have been more excited when our lunch break finally came.

"Plans for lunch," Jane asked with a small smile.

I appraised her quickly. Physically she was a pretty blonde, maybe five feet tall if she had the right shoes on, slim but curvy. From what I could make of her personality though, she was a teacher's pet.

She had taken notes, like actually written things down during orientation. I had doodled and scribbled in my note pad. She had been quick to participate

when Michelle would ask a question. I
had done my best to just stay awake.

"I'm going to head home; I don't
live far."

Jane's smile faded. I couldn't help
but wonder if she had wanted to do
lunch together. A year ago, I might have
been quick to offer to eat with her, and
then spend that time trying to preach to
her.

The thought made me frown as I
headed to Antony's Hummer. I had
viewed everyone as either going to die
in Armageddon, or someone to be
saved and preached to. I was so
blinded.

As I drove home, I thought about
all of the hours, days, weeks, and years,
that I had wasted in the preaching work.
Two things brought me a small bit of
solace, one being that I had never
brought anyone into the cult, meaning
that I didn't need to feel guilty. And two, I
had spent most of that time preaching
with Rebecca.

Rebecca. My closest friend for so
long, now I haven't spoken to her in
weeks. My closest friend who apparently
had been secretly in love with me. My
closest friend whom I just wanted to

hug, curl up next to, and watch a movie with like we had done so many times.

My eyes watered as I drove up the driveway to the camper. And then my heart leapt when I saw Rebecca's car.

I practically jumped out and ran to Rebecca. She was sitting in her car but got out when she saw me.

"Hi," I said, cautious despite wanting to squeeze her.

"Hey," she said, her smile weak.

Rebecca looked as though she had lost twenty pounds, her clothes baggy and drooping. Her hair was a tangled mess, and her eyes had the biggest bags I had ever seen under them. She looked like she hadn't showered or slept in days.

"Beccs," I started to say, but she cut me off.

"It's okay, I'd rather not talk. I just wanted to see you. I'm going to be leaving for a while, but I wanted to give you this," she pulled an envelope from her hoodie pocket, "before I leave."

Her speech was slow and slurred, her eyes heavy. I didn't smell any alcohol on her, but the way she was acting had me concerned for her ability to drive.

"Where are you leaving to? Come in and sit with me for a minute, I'm on my lunch break. Are you hungry?"

Her shoulders popped in a shrug. "I haven't decided where I'm going, but Ohio has nothing left for me."

Her words stung. I was still here.

"And no, I'm not hungry."

I closed the distance between us and pulled her into a hug. "I love you. I'm here, always."

Rebecca held the hug, tight and long. "I love you too," she said, her voice cracking as she pulled away. "I'll see you."

I watched as she drove slowly, calmly down the driveway and out of sight.

I walked into the camper and sat down on the couch, opening the envelope she had given me. And my heart sank.

Em,

I want to say first that I am sorry for how I've behaved the last few weeks. You are my best friend, and you are the closest thing that I will ever have to a sister. Thank you.

I know you've lost so much because of your choice to live free of the cult, and I hope that you get back 10x what you gave up. I'm glad that you have Antony to keep you centered and to give you a place to call home.

But I don't have that. I had it in Louisa, but I threw that away the minute that I thought that maybe, just maybe, you could feel the same for me that I have felt for so long for you.

I don't blame you for not, I just wish that I could go back and change my decisions that morning and never put you in a place that you had to choose between me and Antony.

I tried to reach out to my mom, but she told me that until I return to Jehovah she can't help me. Miguel said the same. I thought about it, you know. I thought about pretending, acting like I was sorry for loving who I love, for being who I am. But I can't live that lie, not now, not after being free, if even for such a short time.

I have nothing now. I haven't had a place to live for weeks, I lost my job because I stopped going. I hate my life. I hate my mom, and Miguel, and everyone that said they loved me, that called me sister, that so quickly turned their backs on me. But even though I *hate them, I love them so much it hurts. I just want it to stop hurting.*

I'm sorry. I tried, really tried, to choose a different path. But in the last week I've done nothing but think about how much easier life would be without having to live it. My mom and Miguel say that I'm dead to them, and I guess I am.

I know you care about me, but I fucked that up too, and we both know Antony will never be okay with us being friends. I have no one, Em, no one. I sit in my car, hungry, tired, and dirty, and I cry. I cry until I fall asleep. And when I wake up, I hate that I did. Sleep is the only relief that I find.

I guess one good thing about the cult is that I don't believe, even now, even not buying half of the shit they taught us, that there is anything after death. When I'm gone, I just get to sleep. And that is where my relief is, so that is where I'm going to go.

I am sorry, I know this is going to hurt you, and that knowledge has kept me going for a few weeks. But in the end, you have Antony, you'll have a family one day.

I hope you know, I meant every word when I've told you that I love you.

You mean the world to me, and I'm sorry that I won't be there to share in your happiest times with you, to stand beside you at your wedding, to meet your babies when you have them, to grow old with my best friend.

Just promise me that you'll move on, don't let this crush you. Know that I'm happier this way. The pain will be gone soon, and I hope you take comfort in that.

I love you, Emily Marquette, so very much.

42

My world shattered, like a fragile china plate that was thrown at the wall. I fell back fully onto the couch for a moment, before stumbling to the phone in the kitchen.

I dialed Becca's number, but it went straight to voicemail. I called Antony.

"Hey babe, what's up? How's your first-"

"Becca came by and she hugged me and was talking really weird about leaving and I thought she meant leaving Ohio but she gave me an envelope-"

It was his turn to cut me off, which was just as well because my words choked as I was about to say what was in the envelope. I was about to say that she was saying goodbye for good. I was about to tell him she left me a suicide note.

His words came back into focus. "...have to slow down, what happened?"

"She's going to..." my words trailed off again.

I couldn't say it. I couldn't verbalize what she was planning to do, instead I just began sobbing.

"I'm a half hour away, I will be there as soon as I can."

I guess it was a half hour before he came bursting into our home. I hadn't moved, hadn't stopped crying uncontrollably. It had felt like I had just hung up the phone, and it had also felt like it had been days since she came to give me that letter.

I realized his hands were holding mine, that he was on his knees in front of me, one hand reaching up to touch my face.

Was he brushing hair away? Was he wiping my tears? I didn't know. I looked toward the letter that sat beside me on the couch. The last thing I remember before my world went black was looking at the letter that lay on the couch beside me, so elegantly written in Becca's flawless handwriting.

***

When I awoke, there were flashing lights outside of the camper, red and blue strobing the walls of our home. Antony paced the kitchen, hands on his head, watching as a paramedic attended to me. I tried, and failed, to sit up.

"Easy," the paramedic said, calmly putting a hand on my shoulder. "You fainted. You're safe, and your friend is right over there."

The paramedic gestured to the kitchen, to where Antony now stood a little bit calmer than when I had looked a moment ago. But when the paramedic had said 'your friend', it wasn't Antony that my mind thought of.

"Becca?"

The paramedic stepped back, and Antony came closer. "There are officers outside, they've put out an alert to look for her vehicle. Right now," Antony took my hand and sat down beside me on the couch, helping me sit up just a bit, "we just need to make sure you are okay."

I sat up completely straight now. My head swam, but I pushed past it.

"No, I need to find her. I need to call her again, get me the phone."

Antony didn't bristle at the demand in my voice. "Her phone just goes straight to voicemail. I called Miguel, and he and their mom have both tried to get ahold of her too."

My eyes snapped to his. "Miguel? He's part of why this is happening. He's one of the people that pushed her away, that alienated her, that made her feel like she had no one."

'One of the people', my mind echoed. I was too. I had tried to call or text her a few times, sure, but as the weeks had gone on, I had stopped trying; I had assumed that she would reach out to me when she was ready.

Fuck, I was just as responsible as her family.

"He's on the way here. I'll keep him outside if you want, make sure that you don't have to see him. I can help you into bed, and you can rest while I talk with him and the cops."

The paramedic had finished packing up his bag of equipment. "Your boyfriend is right, you should rest."

I barely nodded an acknowledgment as the paramedic left the camper. I turned back to Antony.

"I…I can't sleep. I need to find her, I need to-".

My words cut off as I tried to stand, and the room spun.

"Come on," Antony said, stabilizing me, "let me get you up to bed, please."

I didn't argue as he helped me up the four short steps and into our bed.

***

I had just begun to fall asleep when I heard the sound of Becca's mom screaming. No, screaming wasn't the right word for the guttural wailing that came from outside of our home.

I ran down the short set of stairs, almost falling because I was still lightheaded, and burst outside. There were still the strobing lights of police vehicles, but the ambulance was gone.

I saw Miguel holding his mother, her sounds reduced to a soul wrenching sob that poured out of her uncontrollably. Antony walked over to me.

"Sit down," he said, leading me to one of the Adirondack chairs that rested near me.

I did what he said, knowing that it couldn't be good; I knew that it had to be that Becca was gone if he was making me sit, and her mom was in such grief.

Antony kneeled before me and took my hands in his.

"Witnesses saw Becca's car drive off the pier in Lorain about an hour ago. Dive teams went down, but it was too late. They are pulling her car out now."

I don't know if I said anything in response. I remember her mom walking over to me, I remember her slapping me and saying something about how this was my fault, that I had led her down this path. I remember Miguel pulling his mom back before Antony led me back into our home, and into bed.

I don't remember much. I don't know if I got out of bed the next day or not, I only know that my life was forever dimmed that night.

43

The next couple of months went by in a blur. Rebecca's family refused to have a funeral for her, they had her cremated and then dumped her ashes somewhere.

I begged her mother and Miguel to let me have her ashes, or at least part of them, to spread somewhere special. Even if I was the only one to attend, she deserved a memorial and a send off. They refused, and I never knew where they dumped her.

I had offered her mom the combination to the storage locker so that she could get Rebecca's belongings, but she told me 'there is nothing that that selfish little whore had that I want'. I tried to find the strength to snap at her for that comment, but in the end I just hung up the phone.

A couple of weeks later, I finally bothered to check my voicemails. I had completely forgotten about my job at Fuerst Mart, and was not surprised at all when they left progressively harsh messages before ultimately letting me know that I was no longer employed.

Antony had been amazing, he had tried everything to get me to live a semblance of a normal life, but despite his best efforts and his undying support, I barely got out of bed to eat or bathe.

Everything felt washed out, like the color of the world was removed and the only thing left was a sepia version. I slept non stop, and if I wasn't sleeping I was crying.

Antony tried, he really tried, to be there for me. But after over a month of me giving one word answers, and barely moving, I could tell he was exhausted from his efforts.

Nearly two months after Rebecca's...after she did what she did, Antony came home from work and after a shower climbed into bed with me.

He pulled me close to him, wrapped me in his arms, and kissed my cheek, my back molding into him.

The closeness that would have made me mad with desire a short time ago, did nothing now. No comfort, no heat, no emotion. I was numb to the world.

"I'm going to go to New Mexico next week."

I heard his words, knew I should care, knew that I should talk to him about it; but nothing mattered to me.

He could go, that's fine. No one stays around me anyway, not my parents, not Rebecca, not her family that was once like family to me, and now not Antony.

I didn't say anything, I just closed my eyes.

"You can stay here if you want, you don't need to pay anything of course, but I can't be here to buy groceries and make sure you get up and eat."

I could probably do all of that myself. Probably.

He climbed over top of me and laid on my other side to face me. I looked in his eyes, but I don't know if I was really even looking or just had my eyes open.

"Or you could come with me. A fresh start, a place with no memories to sadden you, a place where we could make our own memories. We could find you a therapist, we could get you some help, someone to talk to."

"Memories come with you when you travel."

It was a strange thing to say, even to my ears. I knew what he meant, I wouldn't see Rebecca and I going to the mall together every time I went to the mall, I wouldn't see us driving down the road with our music blasting and singing at the top of our lungs every time I went somewhere.

But those memories still existed. And if I made new memories, wouldn't she fade from me? Wouldn't it be real if I moved on?

"Damn it babe," he sighed.

He really was trying, and he had been amazing. Even now, offering to let me stay here in what was technically his home when he left. But I couldn't muster up the emotion to care.

"Think about it," he said as he pulled me back in, bringing my head to rest on his chest.

And I did. As the week wore on, I debated what to do. In the end, I honestly wasn't sure that if he left and I was here alone I would survive. Not that I would do what Rebecca did.

No, I wouldn't kill myself outright, but would I eat? Would I bother to get out of bed at all? I honestly didn't know the answers, and so I agreed to go with him.

"I'll go," I said to him when he woke up the morning before he was leaving.

His eyes brightened, and what little emotion I had made me feel bad. He was looking forward to a future, and I was just tailing along with him because I had no one else. I cared about him, sure, but it didn't feel the way it did before. The longing that I had for his body, for his touch, for his lips, that was a distant memory. I didn't feel anything anymore.

He looked at me with so much love it hurt.

"Are you sure? Because you don't have to. This is your home, and you can stay here, I'll make sure you have what you need, you don't have to worry about working or whatever, if you want to stay you can."

I shook my head. "No, I want to go," I said, even managing a small smile.

He pulled me to him and held me for a few minutes before he got up and made breakfast.

***

The next morning, we were on our way. As the sun rose, and we left Ohio behind, my mood lifted. State by state, I felt a little bit of weight being lifted off of me. By the time we stopped for the evening in Missouri, and he found us a hotel, I didn't feel as numb as I had that morning.

We got settled in the room and Antony went to take a shower. I turned on the TV and put on some reality show as background noise. I heard the water turn off, and he came out, wrapped in a towel at the waist. He was brushing his teeth as the steam from the hot shower he had just taken rolled out behind him.

Watching him, his body still shining with a mixture of the steam and the fresh sweat from the overly hot shower, I almost, almost, felt the desire to take his towel off of him.

I pictured his body under the towel, his cock that I once couldn't get enough of, his muscular thighs, and I felt just a touch of heat in my core. I didn't know how to react to the feeling, and I honestly didn't feel like I had the energy to think about it.

I stood and went into the bathroom as he finished brushing his teeth, and turned on the shower. When he rinsed his toothbrush off and set it down, I turned him around and hugged him. I rested my head on his chest, and he stroked my hair, kissing the top of my head gently.

"I love you, Em," he said quietly.

I nodded into his chest, and squeezed a little tighter, feeling the muscles in his chest tighten as he returned my embrace with equal force.

I felt the heat again start to rise in my core, and I wanted to take his towel off. I wanted to drop to my knees and feel him in my mouth, something that just a few months ago would have been irresistible to me. But, it wasn't the force that it once was.

So instead, I looked up and I kissed him. Gently, just a brush of my lips to his, and pulled back.

"I love you too. Thank you."

He let me step back, but held my hands gently as he looked into my eyes, one eyebrow cocked in question.

"For what?"

I smiled a small, soft smile. "For being patient, for not throwing me away when I broke," I managed before my smile faded and my voice wavered, "for never making me feel broken."

He pulled me back into a hug. "You're not broken. You're hurt. You've been through so much more than you should have had to, and I'm not going to 'throw you away' for that. I meant it when I said I loved you. I meant it the first time, and I've meant it every time since. I can't pretend that I know everything you're going through, but I'm here, and always will be, to support you and help you however I can."

I let a few tears fall before I backed up. I hadn't cried in...in truth, I didn't even remember the last time I cried.

I didn't know if I liked feeling the numbness start to fade or not. Numb was easy, facing the pain wasn't. So instead, I stepped back and took my shirt off.

"I'm just going to take a quick shower, then we can sleep."

The hunger in his eyes at me in my bra, at the body that he had barely seen in months, sparked the heat in me again.

"Okay," he said, kissing me gently on the lips.

His hand slid from my cheek to my breast for just the briefest moment before he stepped away and closed the door.

I undressed and wiped the fog from the mirror. I barely bothered to look in the mirror anymore, I didn't really care what I looked like. My hair had faded from the bright colors that it had been after Becca took me to Louisa to get it colored.

And just like that, I could feel the tears coming and I tried to push myself away from them, back into the shell of numbness.

The hot shower did nothing to help numb me. I soaped up, and my mind began playing memories of Antony soaping my body when I was still me, when I was normal, before I was broken.

I remembered the way his hands felt, caressing over my breasts, teasing my soap slick nipples. I let my fingers tease myself, wishing I could bring myself to let it be him again.

Memories of him turning me around in the shower, one hand on my breast and the other teasing my clit, had me mimicking his hands. Heat rose hotter, and suddenly it wasn't just water and soap making me slick.

I wanted something again. I desired something again. And that scared me.

44

I finished my shower, my desire to go back to feeling numb to everything at war with my desire to feel alive again. I dried off and opened the bathroom door.

The cool air in the rest of the room made me more alert, and the sight of Antony, no not just Antony but my boyfriend, *my* Antony, laying on the bed in just his boxer briefs had me deciding to let myself feel something.

He wasn't doing anything to try to be sexy, I think he gave up on trying that. He was just laying there looking at the little local magazine from the hotel room.

"Are you hungry," he asked, glancing up at my towel wrapped body.

He quickly diverted his gaze, and I felt love and appreciation for that. After Rebecca...did what she did, he didn't pressure me to sleep with him.

He never once made me feel like I had to have sex with him, had to do anything at all really. He gave me the space I needed to heal. And instead of healing I wallowed, I closed myself off and let the numbness drown me.

But I know it wasn't easy on him. I didn't miss how his gaze would glance across me, take in my body. I didn't miss how he would sometimes start to get hard while he held me, shifting himself to try to hide it for my sake. He had needs, and I wasn't filling them because my only need was to be left alone.

I shrugged, and my towel fell. "I should probably eat," I said.

I watched as his eyes lingered a little longer than they had lately, his gaze appreciating my damp curves. More heat built in me.

I turned around, giving him a full view of my ass as I bent over and picked up my towel, staying like that for a few seconds longer than necessary. The small catch in his breath at the sight of me from behind made me smile, and the feeling was strange but welcome.

I stood and went back towards the bathroom. "Order whatever, I'll eat a little of what you get," I said over my shoulder.

He followed me into the bathroom with the magazine. "I cant decide," he said, holding it out to me when I turned to him, "Chinese sounds good, but so does Italian."

I reached for the magazine, but stopped when I saw the outline of the semi-hardness in his underwear. He must have followed my gaze, because he adjusted himself and started to walk away.

I sat down on the edge of the shower, grabbing his hand and pulling him towards me. I stroked his ever hardening cock lightly through the fabric of his boxers.

His soft moan, his quickening breath, the way he placed his hand softly over mine, made me start to feel the distant but familiar raw passion I once let lead me.

I pulled his underwear down, letting out a small giggle as his now full erection popped up. I looked up at him, and his eyes were as raw and wild with desire as I was now feeling.

I slid my hand down his shaft and leaned forward, licking around his head. His moan pushed me over the edge, and I let go of everything in my mind except for the raw need to feel him inside me, and I started by letting him into my mouth.

It only took a moment before he was pulling me up and kissing me, passion and desire in every hungry kiss.

I wrapped one arm behind his neck and twined my fingers deep in his curls, while my other hand teased him from tip to base.

His hands wandered down my body, pausing for just a moment on my peaked breasts before he slid them under my ass and lifted me up. I wrapped my legs around him, moving from kissing his lips, to leaving marks on his neck as I dragged my nails down his back.

The feeling of his cock twitching in response as is rested against my slickness sent a fresh shot of electric heat through me.

"Take me to the bed," I practically begged.

He didn't need any further encouragement, and he laid me gently down, my legs still wrapped around his waist. I ground my hips against him, needing to feel him slide into me, stretch me again.

He didn't make me wait any more, gently easing his tip in and out, rhythmic and slow, each thrust going just a little deeper until he was fully inside. He brought his lips to my neck and began licking and kissing the soft skin of my collar bone.

The slight discomfort after not having had sex in months just added a little bit more of a thrill, making me think back to when he had used me after I kissed...oh god, Rebecca.

I tried to block her face out, I tried to block out the sound of her mother screaming, the feeling of her palm slapping my face.

But like legs that had been crossed for too long, the pins and needles started. Emotional pain that became so intense it was physical. A sob escaped my lips and Antony stopped his thrusts and pulled his body back to look at me.

"Babe? Does it hurt?"

"Yes," I said, my voice cracking and the tears starting to run down my face and into the pillow.

He was out of me in an instant, and on his knees next to the bed. "I'm sorry, I was trying to be gentle, I-"

I shook my head, my breathing getting more short and frantic. "No, it's...not that...I..."

I couldn't finish. Emotions that had been buried for months, emotions that I had worked hard to push away, to not feel, were all rushing back.

The hole that her decision left in my heart, the guilt that I had not done more to be there for her, the anger at her family for abandoning her when she desperately needed them, the pure and unadulterated rage at the cult that forced her to live a lie, that covered up the elder that had abused her.

Black spots crept into the corners of my eyes as my breathing became even more shallow, short and fast little gasps.

What little I could see was Antony's face, the sadness and fear he wore on that perfect face, his lips moving but no sound coming out.

No, that wasn't right, there was sound, but I couldn't make it out; like someone underwater, his words were muffled and little more than unintelligible moans. Or maybe those were my own moans and wails that I was hearing, distant and barely registering.

He took my hand and put it to his chest, placing his own hand on my chest. He looked in my eyes, no longer speaking, and took deep breaths. I tried to mimic his breathing, and maybe I did.

Slowly the spots receded, the sounds that were dull and warbling once again becoming clear. He wasn't speaking anymore. The only sounds I could hear was that of our breathing and my sobs.

He pulled me to him, nothing sexy about our naked bodies closed together in an embrace. There was no heat of desire from either of us, just raw love as naked as our bodies. I had the thought that *this* was what love was.

Sex was amazing, it was something that was better than I ever could have imagined even six months ago. The night the island with the waitress, the waitress who's name I couldn't even remember now. That night was amazing. But it was carnal.

This, me at my lowest, broken and hurting and wanting to shrink back into a shell of numbness, while Antony held me, while he showed me that nothing was more important to him than me, that even when I couldn't find it in me to love myself, he would love me for both of us.

And damn if that wasn't better than anything I ever experienced in the cult. My last thoughts as I fell asleep, breath still stuttering from my emotional release, was that despite all of the pain I had gone through since leaving the Jehovah's Witnesses, I felt more loved now than I ever had; loved without exception, without condition, without a caveat. I was loved for me, for all of me.

45

The next morning I woke up to an empty bed, steam rolling out from the bathroom door that Antony had left cracked open before he got in the shower.

My eyes were puffy, and I had one hell of a headache. But the heartache that racked me so completely last night was dull this morning.

I wasn't numb; feeling seemed to have returned to me, emotions awake and aware. Love for the man in the shower, pain, sadness, and loss at the thought of Rebecca. But also more.

Love for her as well. Past the pain, past the anger at her choice, I felt love for her. I enjoyed the feeling, let the memories of her run through my mind.

Thoughts of her and I led to thoughts of time spent with our parents, nights spent at each other's house. Beneath the mountain of pain and resentment lied an ocean of happy memories.

Memories of us, memories of my family, memories of Miguel. Pain, loss, mourning, yes. But love, happiness and joy.

I hadn't heard the shower turn off, and I hadn't registered Antony standing next to the bed.

"Em," he said my name with a question in his tone, and I could tell it wasn't the first time he had tried to get my attention.

"Sorry," I said, sitting up in the bed and pulling the thin motel blanket over me.

"It's okay. I'm going to head down to the continental breakfast, do you want something?"

I wasn't sure I did, but figured I should eat something at least.

"Sure, if you don't mind grabbing me whatever, I'll nibble on it."

He nodded as he pulled his tee shirt over his head. He looked great this morning, his sweat pants, tee shirt, and still damp hair creating a nice image. I must have been smiling, because he smiled back a bit sheepishly.

"What," he asked, glancing at his outfit before looking back to me.

I shrugged like it was nothing, but the truth was I was feeling the desire to have him come rushing back.

"Just thinking that you looked like a good breakfast."

His smile deepened, and his eyes went hungry. "Well, maybe you can have me for dinner. We have to get a decent start this morning so we can make it in time to sleep in our new bed tonight."

I let the blanket go and got up onto my knees on the bed, pulling him to me. His eyes glanced to my bare breasts as I did, and it took everything to honor his wishes when I saw the fire in his gaze. I kissed him, being sure to let my hands wander, before pushing him away playfully.

"Fine, go get some food then and I'll take a shower so we can go."

By the time I took a quick shower he had returned with the basic foods that the hotel had.

"I got you some muffins," he called to me through the bathroom door.

Last night had been difficult, but I still wanted him.

I opened the door and stepped out, the only thing covered on my body was my towel wrapped hair.

"I have something better than muffins you can eat," I said, grinning at my terrible line.

His eyes traced every inch of my curves, up and down slowly.

"Definitely better than the stale muffins they had," he smiled as he walked to me and pulled me to him.

I let out a small whimper as lips found my peaked breasts, and his fingers found my wet core. I pulled his face up and kissed the spot on his neck that I knew drove him crazy. I was rewarded with a finger slipping gently inside of me. I moved my hips, grinding against his finger as he slipped in a second one.

"Fuck, babe, you're so fucking wet."

The husky whisper of his voice drove me wild and I slid my hand to the waist of the sweat pants he had put on to get breakfast. Slowly, achingly slowly even for me, I slid my hand under the waistband and down, down, down, until my finger tips found his base.

"I've missed this," I said as I wrapped my hand around him.

He took his fingers from me and brought them to his lips. "I've missed all of this, but I've missed the way you taste the most."

I watched as he licked me off of his fingers, before I kissed him. My patience was gone, I had nothing but hunger for him now. I pushed him back, and laid down on the bed, spreading my legs and teasing my clit.

"Then why aren't you eating me?"

That was all it took for him to drop to his knees and pull me to the edge of the bed.

He started off slow, teasing my wet slit with his tongue. I dug my fingers into his hair and thrust my hips against his mouth. Moments later I was coming, and fuck if it wasn't exactly what I needed.

I pushed his head away, rolling over. "I need you inside of me."

As he entered me, my mind went blank to everything except the pure pleasure of his rhythm, hard and fast as his hips slammed into my ass. I reached back and grabbed his hand.

"Pull my hair."

He didn't need convincing, and soon we were both lost in the passion.

After another shower, and it was not a quick one once he stepped in with me, we finally left the hotel, only a few hours later than when he wanted to but I don't think either of us minded.

46

I held Antony's hand as we drove through states that I had never been too, seeing the landscape morph and change as we went. I fell asleep briefly, but dreamed of Rebecca.

My heart broke when I woke up and could still hear her voice echoing out of my dream for just a moment. How long until I couldn't remember her voice?

"Can we stop at the next truck stop, please," I asked, trying to not let the pain that threatened to embrace me latch on.

Antony reached across and rested his hand on my thigh, not taking his eyes off of the road.

"Yeah, the last sign I saw said there was one in about ten miles."

Antony pulled into a parking spot and we got out and stretched. He looked at me and smiled.

"I needed a good stretch anyway. I'm going to grab snacks, I'll wait for you to check out."

I came around the car and gave his cheek a quick kiss before going in to use the restroom. When I walked out of the restroom I noticed the cork board they had on the wall in the hallway. Business cards for everything from truck servicing to construction to catering.

And right at the bottom, two Jehovah's Witness tracts. Ones that I had read, ones that I had distributed, ones that I had believed. Now I only saw propaganda. I only saw lies. I only saw death and sadness.

I pulled them off the cork board and tossed them in the trash; the idea of someone mourning and seeing a 'What Hope For Dead Loved Ones" tract, finding false hope in the words, and being sucked into a cult that would ruin their lives disgusted me.

Reading seemed like a good distraction though, so I went to browse the magazines and paperbacks. One caught my eye, some shirtless cowboy and a bikini top with jean short shorts wearing cowgirl; 'Hot Country Nights' seemed as good as any choice, and I headed to meet Antony to pay.

Antony glanced at the book and chuckled. "Should I get me one of them there cowboy hats, ma'am," he asked with a ridiculous country drawl.

"Hmm, maybe," I said, before getting a big smile. "Or maybe I should just find us a cowboy to have some fun with."

His eyes darkened and he leaned down to my ear. "You want a cowboy to fuck you while you suck me?"

His voice was husky, and the whisper sent a shiver of lust down my spine. I slipped my hand over the outline of him in his shorts and gripped softly.

"Maybe I want a cowboy to fuck my ass while you are buried in *your* cunt."

He let out a soft moan and I pecked his cheek with a quick kiss again, before spinning and heading to the register. I did not fail to notice the way his cock was pressed into me, half hard when he stood behind me in line.

He wrapped his arms around my waist as we waited for the people in front of us to pay, and I pushed my hips back against him, grinding ever so slowly.

As his fingers teased just under the edge of the waistband on my shorts, it was our turn to pay. I gave him one more grind and went to the car while he bought our stuff.

By the time Antony got back to the Hummer, I had grabbed a blanket from the backseat and laid it over my legs.

"Are you going to read me the book while I drive," he asked with a playful smile.

"I hadn't planned on it," I smiled back. "Do you want me to?"

He shrugged. "Maybe. I'm not sure if that will help me be more alert, or bore me to death with the cheesy smut."

I side eyed him as he put the car in gear and pulled out from the parking lot.

"Cheesy? How do you know it wont be a literary masterpiece?"

"From the rack of a truck stop book shelf? I'm going to make an educated guess."

I reached over and laced his fingers in my lap as he merged onto the highway.

"Are you having a hard time staying awake? I can always take over driving for a bit."

"I'm okay, just gets boring after a while. But if you read to me maybe I'll stay alert."

I slipped his hand under the blanket. "Maybe I can find a better way to keep you alert?"

The small gasp he let out as I slid his hand down my bare body, my shorts on the floor behind his seat, and held his hand to my wetness was like gasoline on my fire. I moved his fingers, circling my clit and sliding them up and down my wet slit.

"Fuck babe, you're going to make me crash."

I paid no attention to his words as I led his finger to my opening before letting go of his hand. "Make me come."

His fingers took over, but to his credit his eyes never left the road.

"Do you remember when I first fucked you in the backseat?"

He let out a small moan before answering. "God, how could I forget? I thought I was going to come before you even slipped me into you."

I began grinding on his hand, letting the orgasm build. "I couldn't stop. I wanted you so bad. I wanted all of you inside of me, I wanted your mouth on my nipples as I felt you stretch me."

His fingers picked up the pace in time with my movements. "And I wanted to kiss every part of you, but god the way you tasted. Fuck, I knew that day that I would taste you every chance I got."

"Then don't stop and when I've finished taste what I've done to your fingers."

He didn't stop, and a moment later I let go of what was building, jumping over the edge and coming on his hand.

He slowed in time with me, his touch becoming increasingly soft until his fingers were no longer on my skin; looking me in the eyes for just a second, he sucked me off of his fingers.

I needed to kiss him. Slipping from under the blanket, I got on my knees in the seat and kissed him. I didn't let it last long, just long enough for our tongues to dance for a moment and for me to taste myself. My hand drifted to his very hard cock.

"My turn," I said as I undid the string that tied his sweats on.

"Babe," was all he said. Maybe a warning because he was driving, maybe urging me on. I chose the later.

My ass pointed out the passenger window as a show for anyone that we passed, I took him in my mouth and didn't stop until one of his hands gripped my hair and held me there as he filled my throat.

47

We made it a ways into Texas before Antony needed to stop for the night.

"I can't keep my eyes open," he said as he pulled off of the highway and into a rest stop.

After a stretch and a restroom break, we found our way to a motel. It was small, one of the mom and pop motels that hadn't been renovated since the 1950's. But it was clean, and after a quick shower I slipped into bed next to Antony.

"I love you," I said, but he was already snoring gently.

I was physically and mentally exhausted, but sleep wouldn't come. The returning emotions that I hadn't really dealt with came like a dark storm.

Anger was first. The familiar anger at the cult, anger at my parents for being so blinded that they would turn their backs on me and treat me as if I were dead, anger at Rebecca for giving up, anger at myself for not doing more to help her.

But the anger faded into sadness. It started with the memory of the morning that I took my mom to the doctor. Until that moment I had still held out hope that whatever was wrong with her would be a simple fix. Instead, it was a death sentence.

Tears began as guilt washed over me when I thought about how that very night I had added pain and stress to my parents life.

I looked over at Antony. I felt so lucky to have him, to have someone that loved me for me. But in that moment I wished that I had never met him.

If I never met him, my parents would still be proud of me. Sure I'd be living a lie, but at least they wouldn't know that. I could be there with my mother, help her as she lived out her final days.

A sob escaped me at the thought of her being gone forever. Would I even see her again, talk to her again, before she died? Would I be allowed to go to her funeral? Did I even *want* to go when the time came?

The sadness blended in with anger as it flowed. Not only would she sacrifice herself for the cult, they wouldn't even give her a proper memorial.

My father, all of her friends, they would sit there and think it was acceptable for whichever Elder gave her memorial talk to spend the time proselytizing instead of talking about her, remembering her.

The emotions were too much. I should've stayed in Ohio; I should've stayed numb, numb was easier than this. This was draining. This was too much.

This made me think that maybe Rebecca made the smart choice. At least she wasn't living this hell anymore.

I started imagining how I would do it. Rebecca chose to drown herself, but that sounded too painful. Slitting my wrists sounded equally as painful. A stomach full of pills, or a bullet to the brain, sounded the most acceptable.

I could feel myself breathing fast and hard, could feel the tears, as I visualized myself in a casket. A gun wouldn't work, because then I couldn't do an open casket.

My breathing became even faster as it occurred to me that there wouldn't be a funeral, a viewing, because I had no one that cared about my death.

Sure, Antony would be hurt. But it had only been a couple of months that we'd been together. That was nothing, he'd move on and find someone better for him, someone that wasn't broken.

My eyes went blurry, and I couldn't decide if it was from the tears or because I couldn't breathe.

Antony rolled over, laying his arm over me. The sensation of his touch made me scream. I don't think I said anything, but I don't know.

His blurry form sat straight up and turned the light on.

"Baby, what's wrong," his voice asked, but it was from far away.

"I...I can't do this anymore...I don't want to live...I just want it all to go away...I can't-"

He pulled me close to him. I heard words, but I don't know if I couldn't understand them. Then he was shaking me.

Was I speaking again? I couldn't tell. I think I was trying to speak, but now I couldn't even hear myself.

My vision got even more blurry, before it finally went black, my last thought that I hoped I didn't ever wake up.

***

Of course I did wake up. I woke up to sounds of hospital machinery around me, voices of nurses and doctors.

My eyes fluttered open and I saw Antony there next to my bed.

"Hey, hey," he said calmly, "take your time."

I looked around. I guessed we were in whatever local hospital was around us in, where were we? Texas?

Antony pressed the call button, and a few moments later a nurse came in.

"Ms. Marquette, how are you feeling?"

I glanced to Antony. What exactly had happened? I remember being in the hotel, I remember crawling into bed next to Antony.

"I guess I'm okay. A little weak I think. What happened?"

She nodded and checked the readouts on the machine. "I'll get the doctor, he can fill you in more."

When she left, I turned to Antony and asked again.

"What happened?"

He looked at me with a mix of sadness, concern, and was that anger?

"You really don't remember?"

I shook my head, and instantly regretted it when the room spun.

"You couldn't breathe and you started talking about..."

His voice trailed off.

"About what?"

He sighed. "About not wanting to live anymore."

Guilt rushed through me. I knew the pain that came with that, I've been living it myself.

"Are you sure that's what I said?"

He scoffed, but his face softened a little. "Yeah, baby, I'm sure. It was scary because the way you were breathing and then when you passed out, I thought you...I don't know, I thought you took pills or something and I was watching you die."

The guilt I felt before was nothing compared to what I felt in that moment. I didn't remember taking any pills, but I also didn't remember any of this.

"I don't think I did. I'm sorry."

He shook his head. "You didn't. They pumped your stomach."

"I'm sorry," I repeated.

"What's going on, Em? I thought you were doing better? I thought this fresh start was helping. I should've stayed home, we should've dealt with all of this. I'm sorry."

"No," I said, putting a hand on his arm. "This isn't your fault. Whatever happened, I am feeling better being out here with you rather than at home. I don't know what happened."

There was a quick knock on the door and the doctor came in.

"Ms. Marquette. I'm glad to see you awake. Can you tell me how you're feeling?"

As I told him I felt okay, just a little weak and dizzy he began shining his little flashlight in my eyes.

"Can you tell me what happened?"

I shrugged. "I don't know. I remember getting in bed, but then I woke up here."

He nodded. "Your friend was concerned you may have taken substances to try to end your life?"

I shook my head. "I wouldn't do that. I don't know what happened, but I wouldn't do that. And we don't have anything to take anyway."

He nodded again. "Well your tox screens came back clean. Are you having thoughts of harming yourself or others?"

I answered without hesitation. "No. I would never do that. My best friend…"

"Her best friend committed suicide a few months ago," Antony finished for me when my voice wavered.

The doctor nodded. "I have no reason to put you in a 72 hour hold for evaluation, but I do suggest that you see a professional to help you through. From what I can tell you had a panic attack, and whatever brought it on could be triggered again if you don't resolve it. I would like to keep you for a few more hours to make sure you're strong enough to go, but I can't force you."

I shook my head. "No, we are in the middle of moving across the country, and I've already set us far enough behind."

"Baby, it's okay to delay a little if it means making sure you're okay. I don't want you to push yourself."

I waved away his concern. "I'm fine, or I will be anyway. Let's just get to our new place and I can rest there."

The doctor said that he'd have the nurse come in with my discharge forms and left.

"We really don't need to rush," Antony reiterated.

I took his hands. "Honestly, I'll be fine."

He nodded though he didn't look convinced. But two hours later, after being discharged and getting our belongings from the motel, we were on the road again.

48

Six Months Later

I sipped my morning coffee looking out over the backyard. New Mexico had been a nice change of pace, but it was coming to an end. The weather was breaking back home in Ohio and we would be going back to Antony's camper soon. Or at least that was the plan.

I had taken the doctors advice from the emergency room that night, and found a psychiatrist. Six months of appointments with them, two a week at first and then once a week for the last couple of months, had helped me tremendously.

I was no longer carrying the guilt of other peoples decisions. I didn't hold onto the guilt of Rebecca's choice, I didn't hold onto the guilt of my parents choice to cut me out of their life for their own religious bigotry.

I had started to feel guilty about what was to come with Antony, but with my doctor's help I had seen that I need to put myself first.

Antony was an amazing man, and I did love him. But I had only just turned twenty and he was about to turn twenty-eight.

It had become apparent that we had lived very different lives, despite our shared experience with the cult. There were things he had already done, milestones he had already passed, that I had yet to experience.

He wanted to have children, and I didn't, at least not soon. When he had proposed to me a few months ago I had said no.

It was such a thoughtful and sweet proposal, but I didn't know if I wanted to be a wife. I didn't even know if I wanted to be with just him for the rest of my life.

We had fought over it, spent almost two very tense weeks arguing over it, before finally I told him to ask me again in a couple of years.

I'd been working for the same company as he did since we moved out here. I had managed to save some money, enough to set myself up with a plane ticket home and an apartment near the local community college. I had enrolled in the spring semester and would start in less than two weeks.

That morning I had to tell him. Tell him that I was flying home while he drove. Tell him that I wouldn't be moving back in with him when I got there. Tell him that I needed space.

I didn't know how he would respond. I knew that he wouldn't be violent with me, I wasn't scared of that. But would he cry? Would he yell? Would he storm out? Would he call me names?

It didn't matter. In the end, this was what I needed to do for me. Maybe one day we would find our way back to each other. Maybe we could still be friends.

I had thought finding him was the start of my best life. And in a way it was. But the truth was, my best life was about me and right now that didn't include him.

I wouldn't be here, wouldn't have gotten to learn who I actually was, without him. And for that I would be forever grateful. But being grateful for my time with him did not equal owing him more time.

And so when the bedroom door opened and he walked into the kitchen, pouring himself a cup of coffee, I turned to him. Many emotions coursed through me as I prepared to talk to him, but strongest of all was optimism about what the future held.

With four small but heavy words,
I started the next steps in finding my
best life.

"We need to talk."

Other novels by the author:

The Brotherhood of Time: Dawn

The Stolen Princess

And coming soon:

The Brotherhood of Time: Eventide
(2026)

The Rise of the Dragon Princess
(2026)

www.ingramcontent.com/pod-product-compliance
Lightning Source LLC
Chambersburg PA
CBHW011316310726
48973CB00011B/2949